The High Society Wife

Book 5 in The Brides of Little Creede Series

by
CiCi Cordelia

ISBN: 979-8-9918608-4-0

www.CiCiCordelia.com

Acknowledgement:

Writing the Little Creede Series has been so much fun for both halves of CiCi. We feel our combined voice has only grown stronger with each book, and we hope our readers enjoy this latest installment!

Stay tuned for Book 6, The Sheltered Wife!.

Chapter 1

Outskirts of Little Creede, Colorado
Late March, 1884

Richard Blackwood winced as one of the stagecoach's front wheels hit a rut, threatening to bounce him and his traveling companion out of their seats. He steadied the frail old woman dozing next to him.

She awoke with a snort. "What is it? Robbers? Fetch my bag, sonny. By God, my Derringer's loaded." She struggled to sit upright, no mean feat when her toes missed reaching the floor by over six inches.

Good Lord. "Nobody's trying to rob us, Granny. We went over a rut." Richard tucked his grumbling grandmother up against a back cushion, wishing for the thousandth time he'd have been able to escort her in a more comfortable manner. It'd be another year at best before the railroad stretched to Little Creede or Silver Cache. In the meantime, they relied on the coach from Denver's train station.

He gently straightened her flat-crowned porkpie hat, which had fallen over one blurry brown eye. "We'll be there soon, I promise. Do you want a sip of water?"

"Eh?"

He enunciated loudly, "Water. Do you want water?"

"Why're you shouting? I'm not deaf." Granny lifted a liver-spotted hand to her hat and tore it off, flinging it to the floor. "I hate straw hats. Why didn't you let me wear my bonnet?"

"Because when I unpacked your bonnet, you demanded I produce a different hat."

"Don't rightly recall that, Robert."

"I'm Richard."

"Eh?" She squinted at him. "You don't look like Richard."

Biting back on his frustration, he thrust the canteen toward her. "Please drink some of this."

She sniffed at the opening. "I can't smell the whiskey."

"That's because it's *water*," he snapped, close to fed up, his composure hanging by a thread. "I don't have any whiskey."

Granny crossed her arms over her sunken chest. "Well, I do. In my bag, next to my Derringer." Leaning back, she frowned. "No doubt I'll need both my liquor and my weapon to survive life in this godforsaken place."

Scrubbing a bandana over his perspiring face, Richard wished for an entire bottle of anything he could get sloshed on. Why the hell he thought his grandmother would appreciate returning to the bosom of her family . . .

Except it was the other way around, blast it. Because Zinnia Blackwood's family had all left *her*. If anyone had the right to feel betrayed, he conceded it was the tiny, elderly lady slumped against the seat, dressed head to toe in stifling black despite the overheated interior of the coach, her half-boots hanging off the edge like a child, asleep again.

He loved her dearly.

Since Uncle Dub had received word of Grandpa August's death, she'd tested Richard's temper time and time again over the past months. Volunteering to travel East to Baltimore, not only to pay his respects but to collect their crotchety matriarch, he never dreamed the task would've been so difficult.

Nor could he have imagined the lengthy arguments, shouting, conniving, all while trying to endure a Christmas alone with the crabby old woman. Finally she had conceded, agreeing to pack her personal belongings and allow him to arrange for the sale of the house and its furniture.

While the coach wheeled on, approaching the final turn leading into town, Richard hoped his uncle and brother—and their wives—were waiting to welcome Granny to her new home.

Otherwise I'll never hear the end of it.

As Little Creede Station grew closer, Richard peered out the coach window, relieved to see several figures standing under the shade awning Abner Dale had erected last summer. From this distance Lucinda Blackwood's crown of dark mahogany hair glowed in the bright spring sunshine. Richard grinned, thinking his aunt-by-marriage and grandmother shared a similar distaste for hats, not to mention a fair balance of stubborn independence. They'd probably get along famously. Next to Lucinda, Robert blotted his forehead with his shirtsleeve while Dub restlessly shifted from foot to foot.

Not seeing Maggie, his brother's wife, anywhere, Richard figured she'd remained behind at the Galleria where she and Robert resided when they came to town. In her eighth month of confinement, she would be in bed, resting.

Richard shot an arm out to keep his grandmother from toppling onto the floor of the coach as it came to a jerking stop. "Granny, we're home."

Ducking a swinging fist, he narrowly avoided getting his eye blackened. Recalling how Grandpa August often came downstairs sporting a bruise, a reluctant chuckle spilled from his lips. Over the years he'd come to suspect Granny did it on purpose, her way of keeping a semblance of balance in her marriage to the often-tyrannical August Blackwood.

His grandmother snatched up the bag he held out to her. "You making fun of me, boy?"

"No, ma'am," he demurred, coughing away the last of his humor. "Just recollecting on how you sometimes, er, popped Grandpa a good one in your sleep."

"*Hmph.* The curmudgeon deserved it." She fussily brushed at her sleeves. "I suppose I have to greet folks." She peeked out the window. "I see Richard came to fetch me."

"Granny, *I'm* Richard. That's Robert, your other grandson, out there waiting for us." Richard took her arm to guide her toward the coach door, determined to hand her over to his Uncle Dub as soon as he could before he lost his temper or fell over laughing. Either would be a relief.

His grandmother stopped in her tracks and gave him the once over. "You certain you're not Robert?"

"God sakes," Richard muttered under his breath, pushing at the door just as it opened and Dub stuck his head in.

Granny immediately shoved her bag at him. "Here, take this. I might have a penny for you, seeing as drivers expect a gratuity these days."

Dub caught the bag, looking confused as he set it on the ground. "Ma, it's me, Dub." He glanced up at Richard, still poised to assist his grandmother. "She sufferin' from dementia?"

"No, I think she just enjoys a bit of goat-getting." Richard lifted Granny carefully by the waist and passed her into Dub's waiting arms. "It's been interesting, that's for sure."

"Don't talk about me as if I'm not here." Granny swatted Dub's hands away. She adjusted her spectacles as she took in the first sight she'd had of her youngest son in years. "You need a haircut and a shave," she announced. Pinching his left ear, she yanked him down to her level, ignoring his surprised yelp. "When was the last time you scrubbed these out? I could grow taters in there."

"Jesus Lord—"

She cuffed him upside the head. "Don't blaspheme." Her attention wavered as Lucinda strode up to the coach, her plum skirts swishing above her fancy polished shoes. "Who might you be?"

Richard's aunt produced a blinding smile. "I might just be Lucinda Carter Blackwood, since your son convinced me to marry him. I'm officially your daughter-by-marriage. My boys, Harrison and Frank, and my youngest, Vivian, are now your grandchildren." She bent, bestowing a fleeting kiss to Granny's wrinkled cheek. "I can't tell you how delighted I am to finally meet you."

Towering over Granny, Lucinda curved an arm around the stooped shoulders, guiding her easily toward the covered carriage often used during inclement fall weather and overly sunny days. "We've a lovely room ready for you at The Miner Stage House where Dub and I have been living while we put the finishing touches on the house we're building. Soon, you'll be as snug as can be in our new home."

Granny's heels dug in, halting so abruptly, Richard nearly ran into her back. "Our new home? I live with no one lording it over me, missy. Robert, here"—she pointed at Richard who rolled his eyes in exasperation—"why, he told me I'd have a cozy little house to call my own. You can take me straight over there, thank you very much."

At Lucinda's blistering glare, Richard threw up his hands. "Don't look at me. I merely told her I'd been staying at Uncle Dub's old ranch until I take over for Sheriff Coogan. If she's determined to live there, I'll stay with her."

He would have said more in his defense, but a bony elbow to his belly cut off his words as well as his air. "Christ!"

Granny rounded on him unsteadily and smacked his nose. "No cussing in my vicinity, you reprobate. Do I have to clean up everyone's language in this place?"

Richard bit back a smile at his cantankerous grandmother's antics. "I think I'm bleeding." He cupped his nose.

Stifling her laughter, Lucinda caught hold of Granny's arm. "Oh, you and I are going to become great friends. May I call you Mother Zinnia?"

Granny gave her the stink-eye. "You may call me Mother Nia. I hate the name Zinnia." She allowed Lucinda to lead her down the wooden walkway to the carriage. "I expect some sort of refreshment brought to my room at this so-called Stage House."

"Well, of course you do." Sending her menfolk a wink, Lucinda guided Granny the rest of the way, chattering amicably, while Richard watched with fond amusement. Dub and Robert stood there, scratching their heads.

"I do believe I understand why it took this long to bring Ma home." Dub patted Richard's shoulder. "You got my everlastin' gratitude for volunteerin', Nephew."

"Is she settled in?" Richard asked, as Dub sank into one of the rocking chairs on the Stage House's wide front porch.

"Yes, thanks to your aunt who has far more tolerance for old biddies than I ever would."

Dub set his chair to rocking, staring out over the quiet street. "After Lucinda and I married, we took that trip to Ohio to visit her kin. Town called Stanley, if I recall. Small, but a nice place. Never thought about travelin' on to Baltimore to see how your granny was farin'. Didn't want to deal with my pa."

He exhaled, a troubled expression on his craggy face. "I'll likely regret that decision for the rest of my life."

Richard gripped his arm. "Don't think that way, Uncle. It's understandable, since Grandpa August was such a hard one to deal with."

"Suppose you're right." Dub clapped him on the shoulder. "I'll tell ya, as for bringin' her home, I'm right glad it was you takin' on the chore. Feisty as hell, that woman. Don't know as I could've held myself in, temper-wise, if we'd gotten into it durin' the trip home."

"It wasn't easy. She didn't want to let me in the house, that first day." Richard released a snort, remembering how his grandmother tried to slam the door in his face. "Thought I was the Bible-thumping Baptist from down the road, come to try converting her religious beliefs. More than one neighbor told me how Granny stopped going to Mass once Grandpa was buried."

Robert stepped out on the porch and took one of the vacant chairs. "Granny keeps calling me Richard." Worry creased his forehead. "She's weaker in the mind than I thought she'd be."

"Ha." Dub kicked back in his chair, folding his hands over his chest. "Ma knows exactly who is who. Wily old gal."

The indulgent expression forming on his bearded face dimmed. "She's close to eighty now. Might be older, come to think of it. Led a hard life with your grandpa, the miserable sumbitch." He sighed, regarding first Robert, then Richard. "The day I brought you boys to Baltimore, I hated leavin' you in his care."

Robert stopped rocking to stare at their uncle. "We couldn't stay in our house any longer, not with smallpox running rampant everywhere. Once Mother and Father succumbed, it'd only have been a matter of time before we perished as well."

Richard nodded in agreement. "You have nothing to regret. You saved our lives when you came by to check on us."

Recalling the harrowing trip from disease-ridden Philadelphia to Baltimore, he suppressed a shudder. Young and grieving, he'd clung to Robert while Dub drove the horses hard, escaping the city before any of them contracted the deadly illness. They'd brought what belongings they could fit in the wagon, managing to leave hours after the local medical board declared smallpox houses would be burned to the ground.

Thank God Dub had gotten them away before they'd had to witness the layers-out, carrying their parents' corpses away. Only the charcoal markings on their wrapped bodies—identifying them as Melvin and Esther Blackwood—would have separated them from the rest of the dead, heaped in wooden wagons headed to a common pyre.

It had broken Richard and Robert's hearts to know there'd be no grave to visit.

Showing up in Baltimore, huddled together on their grandparents' front porch, was a shock. But in spite of his cold, harsh ways, August Blackwood took them in. A month later, when Dub left for the mines out West, Richard didn't begrudge him the choice he'd made.

Grandpa August had always ridden Dub the worst.

"Did he really push you into seminary, the same as he tried to do to us?" Robert inquired. "We toured it once." He grimaced. "Horrible."

"I spent a year there, boys. I'd have been, oh, maybe sixteen, seventeen. Your pa had already moved to Philadelphia and met your ma. He'd sent a letter or two, mentionin' the weddin' they'd had at the courthouse. I think your grandpa was so angry Melvin had left, he turned all his priesthood hopes on me. Your granny tried to talk him out of sendin' me, but there wasn't any talkin' to my pa when church fever got into him. If I'd stayed through to graduatin', I'd be Father Duncan now." He blew out a breath that fluttered his mustache. "Never would've gotten the chance to meet and marry your darlin' Aunt Lucinda."

"Well, I sure didn't regret leaving before Grandpa could send us there," Richard declared. "We asked Granny to come, you know. I hated deserting her, but she told us a woman's place was with her man. While Grandpa was still in church at Sunday Catechism, she gave me all the household money she had and pushed both of us out the front door."

Dub nodded sagely. "He would've found a way to stop you. Though I guess I should be thankful he let you read my letters over the years, otherwise how the hell would you have ever found me?" Stilling his rocker, Dub rose stiffly. "I'm for my bed."

He patted them both on their heads, tousling hair as if they were still young'uns, before making for the front door.

Robert smoothed down his tangled locks. "I'm sure glad you're back." He chuckled. "That little gal who works at the saloon in Rocky Gulch asked about you the last time I rode over to see how the new gambling place was progressing."

"Which little gal?"

"Black hair, dark eyes. Curvaceous as hell," Robert replied.

Richard frowned, trying to conjure the image his brother described, but came up blank. "No idea who you mean."

"You courted her right before you left town to fetch Granny, you fool. How could you forget so soon?"

The memory of a different woman with softly curling sun-yellow hair and big blue eyes came upon Richard so swiftly he choked on his own indrawn breath.

A fist squeezed his heart.

Abruptly he rose, collecting his work hat from the railing where he'd left it earlier. "Told you, I don't recall." Scowling, he slammed the battered Stetson on his head. "Listen, I've got rounds before I head out."

Robert stood. "I'll take the Galleria and half the west end if you can get the rest."

"Deal." He hurried off, ignoring the questions simmering in his brother's eyes.

Richard wasn't yet ready to talk about the woman who'd captured his heart during his time in Baltimore—then crushed it with her easy rejection of his marriage proposal.

Chapter 2

Two Months Later

"Five more miles to Little Creede," the driver called out, causing Evelyn's dread to increase.

Should I have come?

What if Richard turned her away? She could not travel back to Baltimore on her own. That fear had stayed with her the entire trip to this unfamiliar territory. She was out of funds, not to mention too weak to manage such a trip.

Not again . . .

Her traveling companion smiled gently. "It'll be all right, honey. I'm sure your man will be waiting for you when you arrive."

He offered her his water canteen, and she took another small sip, even though she hated feeling like she was accepting charity. She was in no position to refuse his generous offer.

"Thank you, Mister Prescott." She returned his canteen. "You have been so very kind."

"Now, you just call me Tommy. We don't stand on ceremony in Little Creede, and I expect we'll bump into each other now and then."

The elder gentleman had been most attentive to her since they'd left the stagecoach station in Georgetown. Seemingly concerned over her weak state of health, he'd taken it upon himself to be sure she had food and water during the journey to Little Creede. Sharing with her what little he had on him had afforded her the energy to remain somewhat alert.

"I wish I could repay you somehow, but I'm afraid I used the last of my coin in Georgetown for my final coach ticket," she said.

He patted her hand. "Don't you worry your pretty little head. Why, you're about the same age as my granddaughter. I hope if she ever found herself in the same situation someone would help her." He studied her critically. "You should try to rest. I'm sure your husband will be there to meet you upon arrival."

Not bothering to correct his assumption, Evelyn closed her eyes, pretending to sleep as the stagecoach ate up the last few miles to Little Creede.

Yet her mind continued to whirl. Her stomach roiling with both nerves and hunger pangs, she prepared herself to come face to face with the man she'd spurned back home, but whose help she needed more than anything on God's green earth.

Relaxing on the front porch of the jailhouse, Richard tipped his chair back against the rough-hewn log exterior. Townsfolk scurried about, tidying up the street and hanging welcome banners for the Menagerie Museum which was expected to travel through town, sometime soon.

Since returning to Little Creede, he'd spent more time here than at his deputy post in Rocky Gulch. He'd also traveled to Silver Cache for his nephew Duncan's birth, staying a couple extra weeks to lend a helping hand to the new family.

Tucker Phelps, hired on as replacement deputy once Richard took over as the Gulch's new sheriff, was perfectly capable of handling things over there, easing some of his guilt. Helping Granny settle in had been a higher priority, even if she still held a chip on her shoulder the size of the Rio Grande. Maybe she'd find it in her heart soon to forgive her family for neglecting her all these years.

As much as Richard regretted it, what was done was done. Now he'd do all he could to ensure her remaining years were happy, surrounded by her loved ones.

If she'd let them.

Joshua Lang ambled through the open door and plopped down on the other chair, a single encompassing glance taking in the bustling activities of his town. A satisfied smile curved the sheriff's lips as he propped his dusty boots on the railing. "Nice to see everyone having fun in anticipation of the menagerie coming through. It's been a while since Little Creede had a large event."

"I have to admit, I'm looking forward to it too."

Joshua squinted into the sun, blotting his perspiring forehead with the back of his hand. "Gonna be hot the entire time they're set up here. I'm right glad I'll be getting out of town for a bit."

"You still planning on fishing over at Upper Bonney? There's some good trouting in that creek."

"Yep, taking Davey with me. That fool man works too hard."

Davey Bentley had been the Gulch Mine foreman for years, barely taking off any time to spend with his family. If anyone deserved to relax on a creek bed and drop a pole in the water, Richard reckoned Bentley did.

"You'll miss the first few days of the Menagerie," he commented idly.

"True. I expect the family'll forgive me." Joshua shot him a sly look. "You escorting a special lady? If not, I know Vivian has a few friends who'd be interested in stepping out with you. Take your pick."

Richard snorted. This wasn't the first time Joshua had tried to interest him in a woman. "I don't know, Lang, seems like marriage is turning you into a matchmaker."

The man shrugged, appearing unbothered at the accusation. "I respect you, Blackwood, and consider you a friend. I'd like to see you as happy as I am. And there's nothing better than a good woman to bring sunshine into a man's life."

Richard started to form a snappy retort when an approaching stagecoach at the outskirts of town caught his attention. He watched as it slowed, taking the turn toward the station, wheels and hooves kicking up dust.

The coach came to an abrupt stop amidst neighs from the team, Purdy's by the look of it. The grizzled driver ran travelers back and forth from Georgetown and Canon City in the warmer months when he needed extra gambling money.

Keeping a lawman's eye on the stage gave Richard a reason to ignore Lang's suggestion. Besides, his emotions had yet to recover from his last dalliance with a female, and it wasn't something he was anxious to repeat.

Women were fickle.

Spoiled.

Leading a man on with softness and warmth.

Stomping his pride into the ground under a dainty foot.

No. Thank. You.

Richard's focus remained on the arriving travelers. Purdy threw on the brake lever and hopped down, hurrying around the side to unlock the coach door.

His thoughts strayed to Evelyn Calhoun, the flawless beauty who'd spurned him in Baltimore. When the stagecoach door popped open, Purdy held out his hand to assist a lady who looked a hell of a lot like her.

Must be my imagination.

He blinked in confusion, because never would the woman he remembered stoop to travel West to a dirty mining town. She'd made that very clear last time he'd seen her.

His eyes narrowed, straining to make out her features. Evelyn came from money and wore only the finest clothing, her appearance always immaculate.

The way she carried herself spoke of a refined upbringing.

This bedraggled woman wore a traveling gown that hung on a frame thinner than the deliciously feminine curves he recalled, curves he'd loved exploring in minute detail during their time together.

Joshua pushed back the brim of his Stetson. "You know her?"

Richard began to shake his head in denial, when she descended the rickety coach steps. Her hat slipped off, hanging around her neck by its ribbons, exposing a tangle of familiar sun-yellow curls.

Recognition hitting him like a kick to the gut, he leapt to his feet.

What the hell is she doing here?

"Looks like she's sick," Joshua commented, when Evelyn staggered.

Richard took off in a run as the woman he'd spent hours making love to in Baltimore, for a while believing they might have a future together, swayed forward. Tommy Prescott's anxious face appeared in the doorway behind her.

Only Purdy's quick thinking saved her from hitting the ground when the driver caught her around the waist.

Richard reached them seconds later. A knot of tension tightened his shoulders. Joshua was correct, she looked sickly.

"I'll take her." Richard held out his arms.

"She yours?" Purdy asked suspiciously, handing her over. "She puked a lot on the trip."

Richard's gaze fell to Evelyn's belly, protruding from her otherwise gaunt frame. The swell he spotted beneath her travel-wrinkled gown changed everything.

Hell and damnation, she's with child.

There was no doubt in his mind whose babe she carried. He clenched his jaw as Joshua came to stand next to him.

"Yes. Yes, she's mine."

Groaning, Evelyn opened her eyes. Staring up at a wood planked ceiling, she tried to gather her thoughts amidst the hunger pangs rumbling in her stomach.

Where am I?

"You're awake."

At the sound of a deep, familiar voice, everything inside her froze.

Richard.

Her heart raced, blood pounding painfully in her head. Though she'd traveled all the way across the country to find him, understanding she had succeeded filled her with both relief and trepidation.

What sort of welcome could she expect from this man? After all, she'd turned down his marriage proposal.

Then, to show up at his doorstep months later, in a family way? She'd count herself fortunate not to be tossed out and ordered back to Baltimore.

Her hand instinctively rose to her stomach in a protective gesture. Gathering her courage, she turned her head and met his intense stare, inhaling a startled breath.

Evelyn had never seen that hard expression in his eyes before. The tell-tale tic in his jaw indicated his displeasure as he studied her.

Was it a mistake to come here?

After Richard had left town, she'd been devastated to discover she was expecting, terrified at what would happen when her parents found out she'd lain with a man outside of marriage.

Her father, reacting predictably, banished her to a nunnery northeast of Baltimore. He'd intended to place her child up for adoption.

Love for her babe had given her the strength to do what was necessary, resulting in her current predicament.

Evelyn had left behind everything she knew, embarking on a new life with a man she had once refused, and in all likelihood did not want her.

What will I do if Richard turns me away? She had no money left.

Fear rose swiftly inside her at the thought he wouldn't marry her or provide for his child. Returning to Baltimore was now an impossibility. Tears spilled over her lashes onto her cheeks as her chest heaved in a silent sob.

His expression thawed a tiny fraction. "Don't cry, Evie."

The use of the nickname he'd given her only increased her unhappiness. He'd never spoken to her in such a grim manner. Tenderness had always been present in his voice when he addressed her as 'Evie.'

He must hate me now.

Burying her face in her hands, she edged away from him. Her body shook as over a month of traveling, alone and frightened, with barely enough funds to survive, afraid she wasn't nourishing her babe enough, came crashing in on her.

Though she'd refused his marriage proposal, it'd hurt when he left without putting up a fight. She'd wanted him to convince her they belonged together, stand up to her father, and ask for her hand in marriage. If he'd truly cared, he wouldn't have so easily dismissed their romantic association.

Her mind churned, fatigue and heartache causing her limbs to tremble.

At Richard's low curse, her throat ached with the effort to hold back her tears. The next thing she knew, he'd gathered her into his arms and set her on his lap.

Cupping the nape of her neck, he tucked her head under his chin. "Everything's going to be all right now. I promise."

His soft words of comfort shattered the last bit of control she had, and she cried in earnest. If he married her now, it'd be out of duty, not because he still cared for her. Evelyn had destroyed any affection he'd felt for her when she'd denied his proposal. Hurt had flared in his eyes before he turned his back to her and walked away.

All because she'd been too afraid to leave Baltimore. The local newspaper had been rife with stories about the lack of niceties out in the dangerous West. Then there'd been the fear of infuriating her parents, who were pressuring her to choose a man of prestige from within their own social circles. Well, at least her father did most of the pressuring.

Mother never disputed his unfair request. Her lack of support had hurt the most.

As Richard comforted her, the tenseness of his muscles indicated his continued ire.

It'd be a mistake to marry him under such conditions.

But what other choice did she have?

As Richard held Evelyn in his arms in Doc Sheaton's office, her thin frame shook with the force of her tears.

A surge of self-contempt swept over him at the way he'd failed her when she needed him the most. Didn't matter she'd spurned him, he should have found a way to convince her.

Upon examining her, Doc had reassured him the babe appeared to be doing well, given the mother's

weakened condition. He'd left to ask his wife Maisy
to prepare a light meal for when she awoke.

*How on earth did she travel all this way on her
own?*

"Shh. Stop crying now."

Evelyn clutched his shirt, burying her face in the
crook of his neck. "I'm sorry."

"There's no reason to be sorry. As soon as you
get your strength back, we'll be wed."

At his words, her sobs intensified. Knowing she
didn't want to be his wife, and was only here because
of her condition, rankled.

He ruthlessly shoved down the unwanted
emotion. This vulnerable woman, crying so piteously,
carried his child. He'd be a sorry bastard not to do
right by her.

Sheaton's wife entered the room carrying a tray
containing two handled pottery bowls and a tureen.
"Here you go," she murmured, acting as if it wasn't
unusual to find a distraught woman in her husband's
office. "Some carrot pottage from the Stage House.
Plenty for both of you. Spoons and napkins too."

Evelyn peeked out at Maisy over the tightly
clenched fists gripping his shirt. Her sniffles and
tearstained face caused a combined surge of
possessiveness and protectiveness to explode inside
him.

*The woman might not want to marry me, but
there's no other option.* She carried his babe, and by
God he'd be the man raising the child.

"Thank you," came her quivering reply.

He didn't miss the way Evelyn's gaze fell to the
tureen when Maisy set the tray on the table next to
them. Fresh concern for her and the child's health
smothered some of his anger.

Maisy offered her a kind smile. "A nice hot meal
will have you feeling better in no time. You both dig
in, y'hear? I've some soda bread and honey butter for

later, if you feel up to it." Bustling from the room, she shut the door behind her, giving them needed privacy.

Eyeing the thick soup, Evelyn licked her lips, and his body responded to the sensual movement.

Hoping she hadn't noticed, he set her on the chair next to him. Passion had never been difficult for them. They'd rushed from a new courtship into intimacy far too soon. Even knowing the fault lay with him did little to ease his displeasure.

The only reason Evelyn had sought him out was because of her delicate condition, not because she truly cared for him.

Right now she needed sustenance instead of his sour state of mind.

Using the ladle Maisy had thoughtfully provided, he scooped a portion into one of the bowls and arranged it within her reach, adding a linen napkin.

"Go on now. Eat up."

Sending him a shy glance, she snatched the spoon he handed her and began eating, pausing only a second to blow on the steaming soup before shoving it into her mouth.

"Mmm," she mumbled.

Holding back all his questions until she had a chance to get some food inside her, he took a serving and joined her, thankful she was willing to provide nourishment to herself and the babe.

For several minutes they ate silently. A healthy color had already crept back into Evelyn's cheeks as she finished and set the empty bowl on the table.

Yet, sadness etched her features. A glimmer of fear shone in her eyes, convincing him she'd rather be anywhere than in Little Creede. *With me.* She'd said almost those exact words months ago when she'd spurned him.

The resentment he'd managed to conquer boiled to the surface. "I guess I shouldn't make any assumptions."

Richard's upper lip curled, and even knowing he was being a jackass and should shut his fool mouth, he continued, "Are you carrying my child, or did you find another man to fill your bed after turning me away?"

Chapter 3

Openmouthed, Evelyn stared at the man who, months ago, had engaged her affections so thoroughly. It'd never occurred to refuse him when their ardent kisses grew to a point neither of them could stop—or step back from their passion—to regroup their common sense.

"I gave you my innocence." Her hands fisted until her nails cut into her palms. "I gave you what I had never given any other man."

Unable to sit still, she struggled out of the chair, waving away his offer of assistance as she gained her feet. If he touched her, she'd either fall apart again or slap him for accusing her of such behavior.

Richard remained silent, his eyes watchful and his countenance grim.

A glance around the doctor's office revealed cramped quarters. Three steps toward the door afforded her some space, where a window looked out onto the street.

Evelyn studied the busy view while wondering how foolish and impulsive her actions would seem to the man whose proposal she'd refused.

He only asked for my hand over his guilty feelings for our impropriety.

Her own parents' marriage seemed mired in misery and duty, something she'd never wanted for herself.

A feeling of helplessness at her lack of options settled over her like a lead weight. Tamping down her overwrought emotions, she smoothed the wrinkles in her skirts and met Richard's stormy gaze.

"My father forced me to accept going into a nunnery," she stated baldly. "The child would be taken from me and put up for adoption. Or fostering, I suppose."

"Good Lord."

She strove for a nonchalant tone. "He wanted to use me as a bargaining maneuver to climb Baltimore's social ladder."

Disillusionment over her father's selfish actions sent a tremble into her voice. "I'd foiled his plan to marry me into more money, which ruined his chance for greater prestige. I learned he had no intention of allowing me to return home after my nine months of confinement. My fate would have been to either set out on my own, penniless, with no prospects of making a living, or join the sisterhood."

Richard rose, his eyes locked on her, crossing the room to her side. Evelyn ignored the jittery flutter in her chest as he neared.

Coming to Little Creede to find him had been the wrong decision. His cutting statement proved he didn't want her here.

When he tried to hold her hand, she jerked away. "Don't."

"Please." He edged closer but didn't attempt to touch her. "Help me understand."

Some of the tenseness left her shoulders.

For a few seconds they both stared out of the window. Finally, he asked, "How did you escape?"

She sighed roughly. "I stole Mother's household funds before my father had the chance to send me away. Enough to buy Westbound train tickets, and the stagecoach fees once I reached Denver. It was not a pleasant trip," she admitted flatly.

"That was brave of you." He reached for her, and when she didn't move away he took her gently by the shoulders, turning her to face him. "I'm sorry I said what I did."

She blinked back the tears his apology induced. "I regret having to inconvenience you." Her lower lip quivered as tiredness beat at her. "It just, I had nowhere else to go."

"I'm glad you came."

She allowed him to guide her back to her chair, needing to recoup what strength she could. So many questions churned in her mind, she had no idea where to start. As she struggled to sort them out, Richard leaned in and recaptured her hand.

His face settled into lines of resolve. "I have things I need to say, if you'll listen."

From the moment he recognized her, stepping out of Purdy's coach, Richard had ignorantly assumed the worst. Of Evelyn. Of her motive in coming here. Of what made her choose a harrowing, weeks-long trip when she could have stayed in Baltimore where she clearly preferred to live.

Especially after his marriage proposal had been tossed aside with two harshly worded sentences. "*I have no wish to be shackled—out of guilt—to any man. Nor will I live in the wild, uncivilized West.*" With that, she'd stomped off, leaving his honor and integrity in shreds.

Unhappy family situations had drawn Richard and Evelyn together in the first place, assisted by a rekindling of the childish friendship that'd bloomed during Sunday Catechism at the Catholic church both their families attended. Still grieving the death of his folks, Richard had found himself grateful for her shy smiles and sweet offering to share her Bible with him.

They hadn't spoken much in Catechism since the nuns were strict, but her presence helped him during those first painful weeks. When school started in the fall, Richard and Robert were enrolled in a boys' private academy while Evelyn had been educated elsewhere, most likely Notre Dame for females.

Meeting her again in Baltimore after all those years—at the same church during a carnival fundraising event—had seemed like a sort of fate. At the time, her main sorrow had centered around her wish to attend University while her father was determined to see her married to some well-heeled gent with more money than kindness.

Finding out her father tried to force her into an undesired future rang too close to what Grandpa August had attempted with him and Robert. It had created a bond they both embraced as their romance bloomed.

Now, knowing she carried his child changed everything.

He drew in a deep breath and let it out. "Before they died, my parents instilled me with a sense of duty and responsibility. After you and I, well, after we were together, I assumed we'd marry. It was the proper thing to do."

Her back straightened and she frowned at him. "Because you felt guilty. That's no way to begin a marriage."

"Evelyn, guilt or duty aside, I only know I wanted to protect you and your good name. Whether or not anyone discovered what we'd done, it wasn't about gossip so much as doing right by you." He leaned on the arms of her chair, caging her when she shifted away, as if to escape his words. "It's more important than ever we wed."

"Because this is a small town and you risk scandal. Which you cannot afford, being an upstanding lawman." Bitterness hardened her voice as she stared pointedly at the badge pinned to his vest.

Richard threw up his hands. "I don't give a damn about myself! What I care about is you and our child."

Seeing alarm in her eyes at his outburst, he softened his tone. "The babe deserves two parents and a last name. Blackwood might not be anything high and mighty, but it's respected around these parts. I'd like our child—and you—to have it and what it entails."

For long seconds she remained still, searching his eyes, perhaps for some morsel of dishonesty or trickery.

After what her father had put her through, Richard sure couldn't blame her. "At least think about it. Seems to me you came here for support, otherwise anywhere back East and away from Baltimore would have sufficed."

Her stiff expression eased. Encouraged, he stood and reached for her. "Will you let me give you a tour of the town?"

She nodded, grasping his fingers, and took note of her rumpled traveling clothes. "But may I change into something cleaner and a bit more presentable, first?"

After a brief sponge-down in the doctor's examining room and donning a fresh gown from her valise, Evelyn felt much better. The soup had helped settle her queasiness as well as her jumpy nerves, though the walk she took with Richard along the main street of Little Creede—and the looks her presence generated—sent fresh trepidation through her.

A white-haired gent sitting on a wide, shaded porch hooted as they passed by. Startled, Evelyn looked up as he called out, "Ho there, Deputy! That's a purty gal you got on your arm." He saluted jauntily, while her cheeks burned.

Beside her, Richard replied, "Thanks, Hank. Give your own gal my best." Under his breath he added, "Hank Soames. He's devoted to Maude Adams, the oldest resident in Little Creede."

"How long have they been married?"

"Oh, they're not married."

"That's sweet, stepping out at such an age."

He chuckled. "Hank resides with Maude at the boardinghouse. Helps her run it."

She gasped. "You mean they're—"

"Yeah. Living in sin." He glanced at her, amusement dancing in his eyes. "Close your mouth, Evie."

She snapped her teeth together. What sort of town had she'd moved to, where folks lived openly without marrying? Then a smidgen of hope flickered to life. *Will they view my current predicament with more temperance, I wonder?*

"Maude's husband of over fifty years died a few years back," he explained. "The woman vowed to never marry again. Hank too lost a beloved wife, and it almost killed him." His dark gaze lit on her. "You'll find things are different out here. More accepting. Everyone's just glad the two found some happiness in their remaining years."

Richard guided her over the uneven wooden walkways. When they crossed the wide dirt street, she concentrated on not tripping. Ruts, rocks, and horse droppings dotted the rustic thoroughfare, things she was unaccustomed to maneuvering while out on a stroll. Everything was coated with dust here, from shop shutters to hitching posts.

The buildings appeared cramped, the way they all pushed together. Some shared a common wall. Others—including an inn and eatery Richard pointed out, the schoolhouse, the bank, and a sprawling, expensively appointed building she spotted at the very end of town—stood alone.

Finding herself in unfamiliar waters had never settled well with Evelyn. Accustomed to Baltimore and its forward-thinking growth, this small yet daunting silver town would take some getting used to. "Where are we going?"

"I thought you might enjoy a stop at The Miner Stage House." His words were uttered casually, yet Evelyn felt the way his muscles tensed under her palm. "My family's there, probably just ordering supper. You'd meet them sooner or later, anyway."

She swallowed, those nervous flutters returning with a vengeance. Spending time with Richard Blackwood—after the way they'd left their previous association—was a whole lot different than meeting family members who were not only important to him but who would have most likely heard of her less than ladylike behavior and thus judge her critically.

Her steps faltered. "Richard, I don't know—"

"It'll be fine." He tugged lightly, sighing audibly when she remained still. "Evelyn, they don't bite. They'll be happy to meet you."

"Exactly how many *are* there?"

Right in the middle of the boardwalk, Richard turned and took hold of her hands. His dark eyes met hers, warm and steady.

"My Uncle Duncan—Dub, we call him—and Aunt Lucinda have been staying at the Stage House temporarily while they finish building their house. Remember my younger brother, Robert? He's now the sheriff over in Silver Cache. He and his wife Maggie probably won't be there since she gave birth recently and is still in confinement with the babe. They named him Duncan, after our uncle. And Granny Zinnia lives here now."

"*The* Granny Zinnia? The one you complained the loudest about when we were together in Baltimore? The woman you told me was contrary, stubborn, and opinionated?"

His lips twitched into a crooked smile. "The very same."

"Oh, dear." She backed up. "It's too soon. I need more time."

More time?

Richard's attention jumped from her panicked expression, straight to her expanding waistline. The woman carried his child, and though she'd refused his offer of marriage the first time, she no longer had a choice.

He needed to introduce her to his family, right away. Aunt Lucinda and Maggie could put together a decent wedding quickly, with all the details a woman might want. The Carter ladies would gladly pitch in.

In a protective gesture, she wrapped her shawl more tightly around her middle which only emphasized the bump beneath her gown.

Lifting his eyes to Evelyn's, his mouth firmed. He was no expert, but she had to be four or maybe even five months along, now. Time was not on their side, and he intended to make things right. No doubt she'd find him an unsuitable husband, but he wouldn't let it dampen his resolve to marry her by the end of the week. Of course he understood they had taken a chance by becoming intimate, but how could he have imagined he'd get her with child so quickly?

He must have said it aloud, because bright red stained her cheeks, and she gave a quick glance around as if worried folks might be close enough to eavesdrop. Her obvious discomfort made him feel like the country clod she perceived him to be. Thankfully, the sidewalk was momentarily vacant.

"Shush," she admonished, her voice dropping to a whisper. "We can't discuss such things in public."

"I apologize for making you feel uncomfortable. I meant no insult." Richard offered his elbow for her to grasp. She ignored the courtesy as he strove for temperance. "I'd like for you to get to know my family before we wed."

Her eyes shooting daggers at him, she retreated once more. Noting her proximity to the walkway where it met the street, afraid she'd tumble off the wooden curb, he reached for her. "Careful—"

The warning was still on his tongue when her boot snagged the curb as he'd feared. With his heart in his throat, Richard leapt forward and caught her around the waist, overbalancing them both. Staggering into the well-traveled street where wagon ruts caused irregularities and grooves, he managed to steady her.

"Are you hurt?" he began. The sound of hooves suddenly thundered up behind them.

Scowling, he swung her off her feet and into his arms as two riders reined in their mounts. He recognized Floyd and Grover Shaw, peering down from atop a matched set of black stallions. One horse reared back with a snort, pawing the air dangerously close to where they stood.

Arms looped around his neck, Evelyn attempted to avoid the eye-stinging dust by burying her face into his chest. Biting back a curse, Richard hastily moved out of the animals' path.

The twin brothers still lived on an expansive ranch near Cottonwood Springs, won on a hand of five-card stud if local rumor was true. They also owned the smelting works a few miles outside of Little Creede. The two occasionally rode into town for supplies, much to Richard's displeasure. For the life of him, he couldn't fathom how Homer Heath, the man who'd originally built the smelter and employed its workers, would have been stupid enough to enter into a poker game and put up his business as collateral, much less lose all to men suspected of more than a few crimes, as yet unproven.

"Well, now." Grover leaned on his saddle pommel, beady eyes raking over Evelyn in a way that made Richard want to kick his ass from here to Prairie Lick. "Whatcha got there, Blackwood? She your sweetie?"

Evelyn lifted her head, and with a quick glance she took in the two men. Her entire body stiffened as her arms tightened around his neck.

"She's right pretty," Floyd added, tipping his hat in exaggerated politeness. "I'd keep 'er outta the street if I was you. What with all the buggys an' fast horses 'round here."

Before Richard could react to their veiled threat, both brothers dug their spurs into their stallions, making them jump. Whinnying in protest, the horses tore off down the street toward the stage station to the echo of mocking laughter.

At the way Evelyn trembled in his embrace, Richard was tempted to go for his gun and shoot the imbeciles for scaring her. And he might have, if he hadn't been the law.

Even Joshua would have to arrest me for such a crime.

Forcing back his emotions, he carefully set her onto her feet, keeping one arm around her waist. The feel of her body pressed against him felt familiar, felt right. The firm roundness where he knew their child nestled sent a surge of possessiveness over him.

He raised her chin to look into her pretty eyes. "You're not harmed?"

"W-who was that?" Her voice shook.

"No one you need to know." He'd make sure neither of their worthless hides got close to her again. "But if you see them anywhere in town, you stay away from 'em."

"Are they dangerous?"

"They won't touch what's mine." Wanting to offer her further reassurance, Richard leaned in for a quick kiss, intending only to soothe and comfort. It was a mistake. The moment his mouth connected with hers, all rational thought fled. When her lips parted and she returned his kiss, the world faded away.

His arm clasped her closer while his other hand palmed the nape of her neck. When he tilted her head back so he could better plunder her mouth, she clutched his shirt and moaned her approval.

Only the sound of a clearing throat, followed by an amused harumph, managed to penetrate his muddled brain.

A voice he recognized only too well drawled, "Ah suppose yew got an excuse to be kissin' on this heah young lady in the middle of the street under the good Lawd's eyes."

Chapter 4

At the sound of Knight Gleason's thick southern drawl, Richard froze. Surely Evelyn would be upset at being caught engaging in public intimacies. Softening the kiss, he moved his hands to her shoulders as he broke contact with her lush mouth and lifted his head.

The sight of her flushed cheeks, lips reddened from his kisses, sent a surge of satisfaction over him. Though Evelyn tried to deny the attraction between them, whenever he touched her, she'd opened to him.

Every single time.

That knowledge gave him hope. With all the pleasure he planned on giving her, she'd never want to leave his bed, let alone their marriage.

Knight's resurgent chuckle startled Evelyn and her lashes fluttered open, revealing dazed confusion. Fighting a smile, Richard tucked her securely at his side, confronting the annoying yet gallant Galleria owner who'd unrepentantly interrupted them.

"Evelyn, meet Knight Gleason. He owns the local gambling establishment in Little Creede." He paused. "Mister Gleason, it's my pleasure to introduce Miss Evelyn Calhoun."

She cupped one blushing cheek, visibly flustered. "Hello," she said quietly, not meeting the gambler's regard but staring at his vest buttons instead.

Knight's keen appraisal took her in from fidgeting feet to tousled hair, pausing for only a fraction of a second on her stomach. Always the gentlemen, he offered her a kind smile in an attempt to put her at ease.

"Hello, mah dear. It's sho' nice to meet such a lovely young woman."

A wide, friendly grin formed beneath Gleason's fiery red mustache as he held out his hand. Evelyn reciprocated shyly, her narrow fingers disappearing into Knight's large paw as they shook hands.

The big man continued on, blustering yet charming as usual. "Kin ah assume yew'll be stayin' in town fer a while? Ah know my missus would love to meet yew an' introduce yew to the other ladies." With a gallant air, he kissed the back of her hand. "Why, yew'll adore mah Hannah. Best woman God evah put on this great green earth."

Richard bit back a grin and didn't even try to get in a word. The more Knight talked, the less anxious Evelyn appeared, her expression changing to one of indulgence as Knight rambled on, seemingly never taking a breath.

"So, yew an' yer man heah stop by mah Gamblin' Galleria first chance yew get. Supper's on me, an' yew kin meet mah lil' dove. Our boy too." His chest puffed out. "Alexander Knight Gleason. Looks jes' like his mama." He winked at her. "Thank the good Lawd."

His bright blue eyes settled on Richard. "See that yew take good care of yer lady, suh." With a tip of his hat, he was gone, his long strides quickly eating up the boardwalk leading to the Galleria.

Evelyn watched Knight for a long moment before meeting Richard's amused gaze. A smile wreathed her beautiful face, a real one this time and not one offered in stiff politeness. "Oh, my."

His lips twitched. "The man is somewhat flamboyant."

Her musical laugh tinkled in the air, warming his heart. He'd missed the captivating sound the same way he'd missed her touch. The endearing way she fussed with her hair, as if making sure she was presentable for him, whenever she thought he wasn't looking . . .

Not to mention his memories of the breathy sounds she made when he sank into her welcoming body, bringing them both to the heights of passion.

Greedy bastard that he was, Richard wanted more from this woman.

I want everything.

When Richard held out his hand, Evelyn accepted it without hesitation. Striving for inner calm, she let him lead her toward a two-story inn. Painted white with deep green trim, its windows were surprisingly spotless considering the dust level on the sidewalks and in the street. A simple wooden sign, painted to match, proclaimed it 'The Miner Stage House.'

The number of horses and wagons hitched out front indicated it'd be busy inside. Which meant she'd be paraded in front of his family and God only knew who else, only to be judged for the unseemly behavior that left her unwed and carrying Richard's child.

Swallowing down her nervousness, Evelyn straightened her spine and squared her shoulders. *Just another humiliation I have to endure. I should be accustomed to it.*

After all, the one dear friend she'd confided in back home had immediately shunned her. Furious, her father had locked her in her room, intending to deposit her at the nunnery before their circle of friends could learn of her 'sinful conduct,' his exact words.

Approaching the front of the establishment, Evelyn faltered.

Richard paused, squeezing her hand comfortingly. "Everyone's going to love you."

Fidgeting, she wet her dry lips. "What have you told them about me?"

He shook his head. "Nothing."

Nothing?

Like tossing a lit matchstick onto dry timber, sadness burned away her embarrassment. Richard hadn't cared enough to even mention her. That knowledge settled deep within her soul, and a hot rush of tears flooded her vision.

She suddenly felt very weary, far older than her twenty years. Disheartened, she felt her shoulders slump with the weight of her sorrow. "Perhaps I should meet your family at a later time."

As in never.

She tried to extricate herself from Richard's grasp, but his grip only tightened. The urge to flee, to leave him and his little town far behind, slammed into her with a staggering force.

Her initial instinct had been right. *I made a mistake coming here.* She tensed, poised to run the first chance she got.

For the love of her child, she'd escaped the only home she knew to marry a man not of her parents' choosing. A man who hadn't wanted her enough to stand up to her father and ask for her hand in marriage. Instead, he'd returned to Little Creede and broke her heart.

I'd be better off in the nunnery. Except she'd never agree to give up her babe.

As if reading her thoughts, Richard swept an arm around her waist and brought her close. His other hand stroked her cheek. "Evie, look at me."

With a fortifying breath, she lifted her head to meet his penetrating stare, aware of how her rounded stomach pressed into his abdomen. The tiny little flutter, from deep within, had become a stark reminder of the life they'd created together. "What?"

"I didn't talk about what we shared, not because I didn't care, but because it hurt too much to dwell on. You sent me away, and I was trying to honor your wishes." His brows furrowed. "A mistake. We should have wed after our first night together."

"Why? You don't love me."

"I care for you, Evie. That's enough for now."

A smidgen of hope unfurled inside her. "You really believe that?"

"I do." A grin flashed across his handsome face. "One of these days, I'll give you a history lesson on all the unconventional marriages that've taken place in Little Creede. And the couples are all deliriously in love, sometimes nauseatingly so." His seductive chuckle quickened her blood. "Now, let's go inside so I can introduce you to my family and get some real food inside you."

"Very well." She took the arm he offered her, feeling a little more settled. Matching his stride, they climbed the steps leading to the shadowy front porch and entered the building.

An older, beautiful woman came over to greet them. "Richard, right on time. Dub and I just seated Mother Nia." She turned a brilliant smile toward Evelyn. "You're new in town, I'd wager. Did you arrive on today's stage?" When Evelyn nodded, the woman held out a slender hand. "I'm Lucinda Blackwood."

"Lucinda's my aunt," Richard informed her, "since she finally agreed to marry my Uncle Dub, putting the poor man out of his misery." Humor laced his voice, and Evelyn assumed there was an entertaining story behind his words. "She's also the hostess for the Stage House."

"A pleasure to meet you, ma'am." She shook the woman's hand. "I am Evelyn Calhoun—"

"From Baltimore, and soon to be Evelyn Blackwood," Richard broke in, much to her dismay.

Evelyn bit back the urge to rebuke his statement. Nothing had been settled between them. The man hadn't asked her to marry him, only assumed.

Knowing she had no real alternatives made her feel powerless in her life's choices.

His aunt's gaze flicked to Evelyn's waistline for a short second before she bestowed another friendly smile. "Ah, I see. Well, that's wonderful news. Welcome to the family, sweetheart." She clasped Evelyn's free hand between soft, warm palms. "You'll find the Blackwood clan to be a loving and honorable bunch."

Releasing her, Lucinda waved for them to follow her. "C'mon. I can't wait for the family to meet you. They'll be thrilled Richard found himself such a charming young lady."

Keeping her eyes straight ahead, Evelyn followed the elegant woman into a dining salon that held few empty tables. She started to adjust her shawl to cover her stomach but quickly dropped her arm back to her side. It was time she stopped caring about being judged by others. If Little Creede was to be her home now, and these people her new family, they'd have to accept her as she was, imperfections and all.

An ancient-looking crone, garbed in black, sat at a table at the center of the room. *Zinnia Blackwood, to be sure.* A burly older gentleman to her left could only be Richard's Uncle Dub. The facial similarities were remarkable, even underneath the man's salt-and-pepper beard.

The cacophony of chattering voices dwindled to mere whispers, all eyes turning their way as they crossed the room. Finally, after what seemed like an eternity under various watchful stares, they reached the table holding Richard's kin.

I'll no doubt be the talk of the town by the end of the day.

Richard's grandmother studied Evelyn with an unreadable expression. Shrunken in body, the way old people often appeared, this matriarch of the

Blackwoods could still prove more formidable than all the rest put together.

Breaking into a huge smile, his uncle stood to greet them. "'Bout time you showed up, boy." His focus shifted to her. "Hello. I'm Dub, Richard's uncle." He offered a short but charming bow.

"Evelyn Calhoun," she murmured, relieved when Richard didn't interrupt a second time, grateful no one had mentioned her delicate condition, though they had to have noticed. "I just arrived from Baltimore," she added, feeling suddenly defiant.

Let them think what they will of that.

Aside from a brief glance at Richard's set face, Dub's expression remained friendly. "My hometown," he rumbled, patting her shoulder before he sat back down.

Richard held a chair out for her across from his uncle. As she took her seat, Zinnia Blackwood eyed her assessingly. "Girl, is that my great-grandchild you're carrying? When's the wedding?" She spoke far too loudly, the way those with hearing issues often did.

Heat burned Evelyn's cheeks as an awkward silence descended upon the room.

"Granny," Richard muttered, dropping into the chair next to Evelyn, "that's inappropriate as hell."

"What?" she asked innocently, her tone indicating she knew exactly what her words had churned up.

The drone of silence resumed as diners went back to their meals. Deciding it was time to take control of the situation, Evelyn lifted her head to stare across the table at the old woman, expecting to see contempt in her faded brown glare. Instead, she found challenge in the astute regard, a silent 'stand up for yourself.'

Evelyn's tension eased, followed by a grudging respect for the eldest Blackwood.

Time to master my own circumstances.

Shrugging one shoulder, she quirked a brow in challenge. "Your grandson hasn't properly asked me yet."

"Good Lord." Dub smacked Richard upside the head. "What's the matter with you?"

Rubbing his ear, Richard shoved back his chair. The twinkle in his dark eyes belied his serious mien as he sank to one knee at her feet.

Evelyn's mouth dropped open.

Low laughter and excited chatter rose in the air as nearby diners caught on to the public display. Dimly she heard silverware clatter on china plates, those patrons making no secret of their eavesdropping.

Frozen in her seat, Evelyn fought for composure. "I didn't mean right here and now," she whispered frantically.

Richard took her hand between both of his. "Miss Calhoun." His voice ricocheted through the room, making her heart pound hard. She tried to swallow but her throat had dried to the consistency of sand.

Bringing her hand to his lips, he kissed her ring finger. "Would you do me the great honor of becoming my wife?"

"I-I . . ." she stammered, staring at him, while murmurs of approval broke out around their table. Perspiration prickled down her spine at how quiet the entire salon had grown, as if everyone present had some sort of stake in her reply. Forcing her eyes from his, she peered wildly at his relatives.

Dub Blackwood winked at her. At his side his wife nodded encouragingly. Helplessly, Evelyn latched on to the family member whose opinion, she knew, mattered the most.

Zinnia Blackwood's scowl drew her white brows together fiercely. "Well, my girl? Are you going to make an honest man of my grandson?"

"Mother Nia, for heaven's sake," Lucinda admonished. As her husband barked out a laugh, she pushed at his brawny shoulder.

"I ain't got all day, missy. Either you want him or you don't." She leaned forward on her chair, almost toppling from it. "If I were you, I'd be wanting him. Seeing as you've already had him a few times." With a snicker, the elderly woman gestured toward her thickening waistline.

Evelyn's gasp ricocheted loudly in the dead-quiet room.

A woman seated at the nearest table uttered, "Lordy," loudly enough to cause more than one responding chuckle from others within earshot.

Ignore it, ignore it. But that was easier said than accomplished, when sounds of amusement broke out all around.

Dub coughed and jumped to his feet. "Ma, let's get you outside for some fresh air." He carefully gripped her fragile elbow. Lucinda caught her other arm. Between them they maneuvered her out of the chair and guided her away amidst her grumbling protests.

Blinking rapidly to stave off the emotion threatening to choke her, Evelyn returned her shaky attention to Richard, still on his knees. He laid her palm against his chest and held it there, right over his heart.

"She means well," he began.

"I know she does." There wasn't much else Evelyn could say. Suddenly she was envious at the kind of love and pride the Blackwoods all seemed to have with each other, something she'd never in her life been able to claim for herself.

If I marry him, I'll be a Blackwood too.

Meeting the deep brown gaze of the man she'd traveled almost two thousand miles to find, she felt her insides settle. "Ask me again."

Fresh murmurs broke out as diners closest to their table watched avidly, the woman who'd exclaimed aloud earlier now sighing, "How romantic."

At the visible tenderness in Richard's gaze, Evelyn had to agree.

Still holding her palm to his chest, he reached with his other hand and stroked her cheek. "Evelyn, will you marry me?"

Her heart pounding at the life-altering question, she produced the only sensible response. "Yes."

Chapter 5

A week had flown by awfully fast, with Evelyn's health drastically improving. Richard made sure she got three solid meals a day. She had the appetite of a horse and no longer worried about the babe getting enough nourishment.

It would have been mortifying if not for the reassurances of Richard's aunt who explained such food craving was completely normal since Evelyn was eating for two.

Chewing on her lower lip, she stared into the full-length mirror Lucinda had brought into one of the Stage House rooms for her use. The gown *was* lovely. With pale blue silk banded in deeper cobalt trim, the color somehow accentuated the brightness of her eyes.

She ought to be impressed at how quickly a wedding could be put together in mere days, but she was too apprehensive about the upcoming nuptials.

Mostly, she felt sick to her stomach, something else Lucinda had promised would eventually ease.

Downstairs, a salon had been allocated for the ceremony with a brief reception to follow. Yesterday at supper, the Stage House's beautiful owner, Catherine Carter, had introduced herself and smilingly volunteered the use of her tea salon, adding a light repast befitting a wedding reception would also be provided.

Before Evelyn's head could stop spinning at such generosity, the last remaining, unintroduced Blackwood—Maggie, Robert's wife—came over to the table. She'd enveloped Evelyn in a perfumed hug, kissed her cheek, and whispered, "I always wanted a sister."

The genuineness of those words had helped settle some of Evelyn's anxiety.

Her future sister-by-marriage had held out a linen wrapped package. "I wore this gown during my confinement with Duncan. I'm sure it will look perfect on you."

Evelyn turned to the side, adjusting the gathering which allowed for an expanding waistline. Delicate ivory lace spilled down the high-neck bodice with faceted sapphire buttons sparkling amidst the froth. Three-quarter sleeves, loose and comfortable, ended in more lace, and the back boasted a pleated day-train. Bands of lace embellished the hem all around. She couldn't imagine a prettier wedding gown.

Weariness suddenly weighed her down as she returned to rest on the vanity chair. Longing to nap, if only for a moment, she eyed the bed taking up one corner of the room, draped in soft green fabric.

No, she silently scolded. *If I crawl in bed now, I'll never get up again.*

Smoothing one hand over her hair, it dawned on her she'd forgotten to do anything with it for the ceremony. Sighing, she struggled back to her feet just as a knock sounded.

"What now?" She forced herself to walk to the door and open it.

Zinnia Blackwood stood there, dressed in funeral black, hair braided and wreathed around her head like a crown of silver. Bespectacled eyes sharp as a darning needle swept over her from tangled curls to her travel-worn half-boots, the only shoes she owned. "Well?" she demanded. "You going to invite me in?"

Moving to the side, she allowed the elderly matriarch entry. Hobbling a bit, gnarled fingers gripping her cane, she advanced to the center of the room. "Bring me a chair, girl."

Evelyn cast about for anything resembling a decent chair and came up empty. "I can get one from another room—"

"That frilly seat yonder will suffice. I'm not an invalid."

Dragging the vanity chair over, she hovered uneasily while Zinnia settled herself, propping her cane against her voluminous skirts.

"Come here and let me take a look at you," she demanded.

Swallowing down resentment at being ordered about, Evelyn ventured closer, maintaining the poise drilled into her head from a young age, finding herself examined by a piercing stare that missed nothing.

Missus Blackwood gave a single, firm nod. "Marrying my grandson means you're family now, so you'll call me Granny Nia." She paused. "Well?"

"Th-Thank you, Granny Nia," Evelyn replied dutifully, wondering where this conversation might be heading. She shifted uneasily from foot to foot, fighting against squirming like a toddler.

For a few more endless moments, Granny Nia stared unabashedly, before abruptly fumbling with the collar framing her wrinkled neck. Pulling out a necklace, she held it up, revealing a wide-banded ring hanging from the dulled gold.

"Unhook the chain, child."

Stepping behind her, Evelyn found the clasp and carefully released the fastening. When she tried to pass it to Granny Nia, the woman shook her head.

"You give this ring to Richard during your vows. Belonged to his granddaddy. August meant for the oldest boy to have it." She gestured impatiently when Evelyn stood there, statue-like. "Put it somewhere safe else you lose it."

Evelyn felt for one of the side pockets in her skirt, and dropped the ring in. "I don't—" She cleared her throat, but it felt as if a boulder had gotten stuck in there. "I don't know . . ." Her voice trailed off miserably at the thunder in Granny Nia's frown.

"Don't know if you want to marry?" She shook a scolding finger under Evelyn's nose. "Don't see as you got much of a choice, little missy. You and my boy jumped ahead of the wedding night, and that makes you responsible afore your time." Her eyes snapped with purpose. "You'll wed to give my great-grandchild a name, and you'll do it today."

Evelyn's spine stiffened at the rebuke. She was weary, her legs felt crampy, and her stomach churned. Richard's grandmother might deserve respect due to her age, but she had no right to chastise. "Missus— Granny Nia, I accepted Richard's proposal, but we don't love each other."

The eldest Blackwood leaned in, jabbing an accusatory finger in the air. "You found enough love between the sheets to create a babe, didn't you? Now your fate is set. My boy's no saint, but he doesn't shirk his obligations either." She settled back onto the chair, sitting ramrod straight despite the curve in her spine that indicated elderly, fragile bones. "He'll make a fine husband and provide well for you and your children."

Even as she silently cringed at being called someone's obligation, Evelyn's defiance wilted. Granny Nia's words were true. "I know Richard is an honorable man. I suppose I'm worried about marrying only to rectify our impulsive actions, instead of for love."

"There's a duty in caring for the making of children, you know. Impulsive or not." The words were waspish, but the palsied hand Granny Nia laid against her cheek held tenderness.

She raised Evelyn's chin. Wisdom as well as irritation shone from her eyes. "You'll do right by the babe. Both of you. Love will come."

Evelyn's lips curved in a reluctant smile. "Your grandson said something very similar to me."

"Well, he's smart, ain't he? Takes after his granny."

Richard gave the room a onceover, noting the special touches of flowers and candlesticks here and there, already lit and glowing. His aunt had instantly understood Evelyn's aversion to marrying in church in her condition. Reverend Matias had proved agreeable to perform the ceremony here, another blessing.

Of course, the good Reverend and his wife were in the dining room last week when Richard had dropped to one knee and proposed to Evelyn.

Robert approached, bumping shoulders by way of greeting. "Never thought I'd see you in anything but dungarees." He brushed imaginary dust from Richard's black town coat, straightening the lapels, then tugged playfully on his string tie. "You clean up decent, brother."

Already unsettled at the huge step he was about to take, Richard swatted him away. "Leave off and go bother somebody else."

"Not until I pass this on." Robert held out his pinky finger. On the very tip sat a dainty gold band, etched with wear yet still catching a gleam from the candlelight. "Granny's wedding ring. She slapped it in my hand and told me to make sure you got it."

He accepted the circlet, examining it closely. Granny had small hands. *So does Evelyn.* In all the rush to organize the wedding, he hadn't thought of getting his bride a ring. "When did she give this to you?"

"'Bout an hour ago. She had Dub help her climb the stairs."

"I'll bet she headed right for Evelyn." He spun toward the door, wondering what Granny was up to.

He wouldn't have his bride upset, today of all days, by any family member.

Robert grabbed his arm. "Hold on, now. She's not gonna stop your wedding—"

"You know how contentious Granny can be," Richard protested. "Blunt to the point of pain." He strode toward the lobby, determined to drag his brother along if the fool didn't let go. Wisely, Robert released him, standing back in a surrendering motion.

Crossing to the staircase, he stopped short at the sight of Evelyn, her tinkling laughter floating down to him from the landing. Next to her, Granny Zinnia held her arm, her other hand fisting her cane.

His heart swelled with pride at the careful way his betrothed guided his grandmother down the stairs. Heads bent toward each other, silver and golden, they descended slowly.

Granny's smiling. It'd sure been a long time since he'd seen her cheerful.

He came forward as they reached the bottom. Evelyn blushed when her eyes met his. Silently she relinquished Granny to Robert, who'd stepped up beside him.

"Ma'am." His brother offered an elbow. "Shall I see you to your chair?"

She squinted up at him from behind her spectacles. "You may indeed, Richard."

Robert exhaled noisily. "Granny, I'm—"

"Yes, yes. I know who you are. I'm not feeble." She grasped his arm.

As she passed by Richard, the old biddy winked.

Smothering his amusement, he turned to take in the sight of his bride. Garbed in blue, she stole his breath with her loveliness. Her unbound hair caught sunglow from the windows lining the side walls of the lobby, making her appear angelic.

"Miss Evelyn," he rasped, clearing his throat. "May I escort you?"

She faltered a bit. "Y-Yes." Tilting her head, golden curls spilled over one shoulder as she touched a silky tendril. "I forgot to fix my hair."

"It's beautiful." He reached for her hand and tucked it in the crook of his elbow. "Ready to get hitched?"

Evelyn visibly swallowed. "We are doing the right thing. Aren't we?"

Questions swam in those pretty eyes of hers. Uncertainty, worry, nerves. The same questions had plagued him too . . . until the moment he'd seen her, walking Granny down the staircase so carefully and solicitously.

The tight muscles across his shoulders loosened. Whatever troubles lay ahead, could be solved. City-bred Evelyn Calhoun might be out of her element this far West, but she'd adapt. She'd find ways to make this life her own.

"Yes, Evie. We're doing the right thing."

She didn't respond further but the way she squeezed his forearm spoke volumes.

Relieved, Richard escorted his bride into the tea salon where Reverend Matias, somber in his black cassock, waited patiently. Robert and Maggie, acting as witnesses, had taken positions on either side. Several chairs, scattered here and there, held the rest of the family, with Granny rocking infant Duncan in her arms.

Matias produced a well-worn Bible from one cavernous pocket and opened it. "Shall we begin?" He winked at Evelyn. "If the young lady is ready."

"I am," she said sweetly. "Thank you for asking."

"I understand you've both been raised Roman Catholic. I can adjust parts of the ceremony to include the proper prayers and sacrament of marriage, if you'd like," Matias offered. "It would be my pleasure."

Richard met his future wife's questioning glance. "Whatever you want is fine with me," he murmured.

For a moment she stared at him, and he would have given anything to know what went on in her mind. Maybe she fretted over the incongruity of wedding in haste, though they'd both promised each other they'd set aside any guilt and uncertainty. Still, years of compliance to strict religious rules couldn't be set aside so easily.

Finally, she shook her head. "Reverend, this is my town now, so I'd be happy if you would marry us under your church's traditional service."

As Matias nodded and began, "Dearly Beloved," Richard knew he'd made the right decision to wed.

Chapter 6

"Truly, Granny Nia," Evelyn protested, as Richard settled the heavy leather trunk into the back of Dub's wagon, "there's no reason for you to move out."

Evelyn hated feeling like she was forcing the elderly woman from her home, and guilt curdled like sour milk in her stomach. "The house is plenty big enough for the three of us. Please, won't you reconsider?"

The eldest Blackwood turned to her with a sly look and a twinkle in her eyes. "I wouldn't want to come between a newly wedded couple. Why, I still recall how August and I canoodled in almost every room of our home. Frequently."

Richard and Dub both groaned.

Dub grasped his petite mother around her waist and lifted her onto the bench seat. "Ma, don't embarrass the poor girl."

Too late for that.

Heat filled Evelyn's cheeks. At the sound of Richard's amused chuckle, she cast him a dirty look. Her breath caught at the familiar gleam in his eyes, similar to what she'd seen back East right before they ended up in bed together, where he'd do wonderfully wicked things to her body; things she never could have imagined but had soon come to crave more than her next breath.

"Oh, Lord," Granny Nia exclaimed dramatically, waving one frail hand in front of her face. "We'd best be on our way, Son. These newlyweds need to start newly weddin'."

She thumped her cane at her own wit, even as Richard huffed in exasperation and Dub bit back a cough as he climbed into the wagon and picked up the reins. "Ma, behave."

He tipped his hat toward Evelyn. "If my nephew gives you any trouble, little lady, you let me know. I'll set him right straight."

With a flick of the reins the wagon rolled away, the sound of Granny's cackles hanging in the air.

Unwilling to look at Richard, nervous energy flooding her limbs, Evelyn kept her attention on dust the buckboard left behind as it drove the nine miles back to town under a rose-tinged sunset.

Married.

The wedding ceremony had been short, followed by a small gathering at The Miner Stage House with Richard's friends and family. Over slices of iced cake, his grandmother announced she'd be moving in with her son and his wife. Since the woman had only a single trunk filled with her clothing and personal treasures, it'd been easy enough for Dub to follow them out here to Richard's ranch house, collect his mother's things, and bring her home the same day.

Leaving me alone with my new husband.

She didn't know him very well despite all they'd shared back in Baltimore. Her desire was another matter, eliciting a need beyond all sensibility. Her babe took that moment to flutter inside her, reminding her of the reason she'd traveled across the country to find him.

For her child's sake, she would embrace the future Richard offered. He was a good man, even if marriage to him would be different than the life she'd always envisioned for herself.

A pampered life of luxury married to a wealthy man. The thought shamed her. Was she really so weak of character? At the sound of Richard's approaching footsteps across the hard ground, she braced herself, letting go of her childish dreams and embracing reality.

"Evie, come inside."

She straightened her spine and turned to him. Caring shone in his eyes, easing her tension. With a smile, she took his outstretched hand.

Together, they covered the short distance to the house and up the two steps leading inside. Brightly colored flowers bordered the porch, leaving one with a sense of peace. The interior held a quaint appeal, considerably more spacious than it appeared from the outside.

"The ranch used to be more of a hunting cabin, one main room and the kitchen area. Dub slept on a bedroll near the fireplace. When he moved to town, Robert and I added on two bedrooms in the back," Richard commented, as he escorted her inside.

"I'd never have guessed," she marveled, unable to tell where the original walls stopped and the expansion began.

She'd peeked inside earlier, while Dub helped Granny Nia pack up her belongings. A sunny kitchen opened into a tidy sitting room where a cushioned chair sat close to the hearth. Bright, hand-hooked rugs were scattered over dark floorboards, stopping in front of a comfortable-looking sofa.

"This room changed a lot." Richard nodded toward the wide mantel. "We split it into a kitchen and sitting area. All Dub had was a cookpot hanging over the fire and a moth-eaten settee. When Aunt Lucinda first saw the inside, she was horrified. She told him under no circumstances was she living here. She dragged him out to her place, nearby the Carter ranch where her son Harrison and his family resides."

"But your aunt and uncle live at the Stage House, don't they?" Evelyn asked, confused.

"Sure, now. But back then Aunt Lucinda had a nice cottage on Carter land. She was accustomed to being on her own. Same as Granny, I suppose. But she also needed to live in town once she took on the hostess position at the Stage House, so she decided to move. Dub came with her. 'Course, he didn't need a whole lot of convincing since he'd do just about anything for her."

He led her through the kitchen to the back door, where—much to her surprise—the porch was enclosed on three sides and boasted window shutters painted a soft blue. At her raised eyebrows, Richard smiled somewhat sheepishly. "Harrison's wife, Retta, gave me some extra paint from when she freshened their sons' room." He shrugged. "I like blue."

"And flowers," she teased, pointing toward the profusion of potted blooms sitting on rough-hewn shelves. Eyeing the shutters, she commented, "Closing them keeps out the rain, correct?"

"Exactly." He followed her as she peered out the closest window, overlooking an extensive garden bathed in the glow of early evening, spotting crops thriving in rows. "I like tater pottage too." His tone held equal parts anticipation and hope.

He's going to expect me to cook for him. It was an aspect of marriage Evelyn had conveniently set aside. Now the thought had her pulse racing. She'd never cooked a thing in her life.

Unwilling to let her new husband see her domestic inadequacies, she murmured, "I'd love to see the rest of the house."

Since Granny Nia had only lived here a short time, she assumed Richard was the gardener. The man definitely had a green thumb. Growing up in Baltimore, there'd been servants around to take care of such mundane tasks as preparing meals and maintaining the grounds at her childhood home.

I hope I don't end up killing all the plants or poisoning my new family.

Overwhelming inadequacy rose up inside her. How on earth was she going to do this?

As if sensing her distress, Richard took her shoulders and turned her to face him. His brows crunched in alarm. "What is it? Is it the babe?"

She had to tilt her head back to look into his eyes. Her body responded to his nearness as it always did. Richard Blackwood was a handsome man.

Big and brawny, he towered over her by a good half-foot, with thick black hair she'd loved running her fingers through. His dark brown eyes mirrored his every emotion.

It hadn't taken her long to learn how to read him, one of the reasons she'd rejected his proposal. Evelyn hadn't seen love in his eyes, only deep guilt and resolution.

At the time, she'd already been partway in love with him. Knowing he didn't return her feelings hurt her deeply. In her anger she'd lashed out, ending their romance, something she soon came to regret even before realizing she was with child.

"The babe's fine." She puffed out a frustrated breath. "I'm feeling out of my depth, if you really must know."

"Didn't you go to Notre Dame? Your education must have encompassed—"

"I learned how to speak Latin and French," she interrupted, shrugging from his grasp. "We were taught how to ply an embroidery needle. How to play the piano and the violin prettily. My learned 'talents,' if you can even call them such, didn't extend to the more practical necessities."

She gestured toward a potted plant nestled on a ledge next to the front door. "I don't know the first thing about horticulture. I don't even know what kind of flora that is." She spun, taking in his utterly spotless home. "I've never had to so much as lift a duster or wash a dish or tidy the bedding. Or polish the floor."

Her throat hitched painfully as a sense of doom beat at her. Evelyn had never been one to doubt herself, secure with her worth in society, confident of besting whatever challenge might task her.

Here, with this man in an unfamiliar little boom town, she felt as if the carpet had been swept from under her feet.

Her attention swung back to Richard who stared at her as if trying to understand why she'd worry so. Instinctively she cupped the swell of her abdomen where their child rested. "How am I ever going to be a capable wife? A competent mother?"

Her voice cracked. "I was taught to act a certain way, to dress appropriately in order to attract a husband my father would deem suitable. A husband of wealth and prestige who would provide for me as well as allow my parents to continue their elite lifestyle within society."

Tears welled in her eyes, causing his image to shimmer. She gestured toward the kitchen where an intimidatingly large cook stove took up most of one wall. "If you asked me to boil water, I'd likely set the room afire. I'm not prepared for this life. What if I fail?"

Richard's expression softened. "I believe in you, Evie. The woman I met in Baltimore is capable of all these things."

Her lower lip quivered. "You really think so?"

"I do. You're strong and resilient." He edged closer, one hand easing to the nape of her neck, lowering the other to caress her roundness. "I have no doubt you'll be a wonderful mother."

"How can you know that?" Her heart pounded hard at his nearness. Her breasts tingled with the need to feel his mouth moving over them again. Heat grew between her thighs at the memory of his familiar touch.

His gaze darkened as his thumb traced small circles over her nape, making her shiver. "Somehow, you were able to find your way across dangerous territory to seek me out. To protect our child. Only a good mother with a heart full of love would have attempted such a risky journey."

"What if I make mistakes?" Her father's cruel words, whenever she didn't live up to his standards of perfection, still tormented her, the reason why she always strove to be the best at everything she did. Deep in her heart, she suspected the fear of failure also stopped her from trying new things.

"As your husband, if you stumble, I'll be there to catch you."

The sincerity of his words was like a healing balm. "You will?" she asked breathlessly.

"We're in this together." He lowered his head, until his lips were a mere breath away from her own. "Trust me. I won't let you fall."

Then—*thank God*—he kissed her.

The second his lips met hers, Richard knew it'd been a mistake. He'd planned to give his new wife time to feel comfortable in their marriage before asking for anything more. Even now, as his body hardened and his heart raced, he told himself to take a step back, but his feet wouldn't obey.

Instead, he tilted her face up to his, bending at the knees to better seal their kiss. With a breathy moan, her mouth opened for him, their tongues colliding in mutual desperation.

Her heady sweetness, and eager response to his marauding lips, overrode any lingering resentment that she'd only married him because of her condition.

He cupped her perfect breast, thumbing the tight nipple. A growl rumbling in his chest, he swallowed her whimper of pleasure. Her arms encircled his neck as she edged closer, the swell of her stomach a reminder of the tiny life she held inside.

As much as Richard wanted to strip her bare and slide between those silky thighs, to reacquaint himself with her body and bring her pleasure before seeking his own release, he knew she wasn't ready. When Evelyn joined with him again, it'd be her choice, not because she felt obligated as his new bride.

I need to prove to her that she made the right decision in marrying me.

That thought applied some needed sanity to his lust-soaked brain. Somehow, he managed to get his passion under control, though he'd never regret touching her.

"Evie, look at me."

Her lashes flickered until her dazed eyes opened and focused on him, desire in their depths. Clasping her around the waist, he embraced her loosely, finding satisfaction in her ready response.

"We have all the time in the world." He kissed her mouth, tasting her sigh. With much effort, he pulled away, staring into her flushed face. "Though we'll share a bedroom, perhaps we should take some time to reacquaint ourselves rather than leap into passion."

She blinked, looking surprised at his words. Then humor curved her lips. "Well. That makes sense."

When she stepped back, he reluctantly let his arms fall to his sides, already regretting his gallantry, even knowing it was the right thing to do.

Longing overcame him as she straightened her gown and smoothed her hair where he'd mussed it.

His heart thumped under his breastbone.

Evelyn had turned down his proposal the first time he asked. Now, given a second chance, Richard had no intention of ruining his good fortune. The noticeable roundness beneath her gown, a constant reminder of his responsibility, only strengthened his decision to give her what she needed to adjust to her new life.

"I suppose you're correct, Richard." Her gaze softened on him. "I never realized what a gentleman you were."

Guilt nipped at him. When their desires had first overruled common sense, they'd never taken the time to enter into a proper courtship. He blamed himself for that lack of propriety since he should have shown more control where she was concerned.

I'll do it right this time. "In many things we are still strangers. How about we start rectifying that over supper?"

She beamed at him. "Sounds like a wonderful plan."

Chapter 7

After Richard left for town the next morning, Evelyn wandered through the quiet ranch house.

What on earth should I do first?

Her life had certainly changed drastically in a short time. Running her finger over a side table in the tiny hall between the kitchen and sitting room, she left a streak behind. "How dusty it is already."

If I close the windows the house will stifle me.

How had the servants in her Baltimore home dealt with dust? Probably one or more of the maids wiped everything down each day, though for the life of her she couldn't bring to mind what they'd have used. Their aprons, perhaps.

Realizing how self-indulgent she'd been, her cheeks burned.

Did I ever give them a friendly smile or kind word, or did I just go about my pampered life?

She searched her memories, relieved to find a few occasions where she'd offered some kindness to her father's household staff.

Peering out the rear door of the kitchen to the back porch, she cataloged the variety of flowering potted plants. Because of the shutters Richard had built to protect them from the weather, these must be important to him.

Hesitantly she touched a red bloom on a shelf right next to the door. A profusion of petals drifted to the floor.

"Oh, dear." She looked closer at the plant, noting how dry it appeared. "Poor thing needs moisture."

Ducking back into the kitchen, she hunted around for something to hold water and spied a spouted can on the floor by the sink.

She lifted the container—heavier than it looked—and set it in the sink, under what she figured must be the faucet. Except there was none to be found. Instead, a thick pipe rose from the surface of the sink, an oddly shaped handle attached on one side.

"Hmm." She pushed at the handle. Nothing happened. "How strange."

She pushed from a different angle. Still nothing. Irritated, she grasped the end of the handle and pulled down, expecting a flood of water. Not a drop emerged.

Why on earth didn't I ask Richard how this thing works?

How was she to obtain the simplest thing such as water, when she couldn't decipher a way to actually *draw* it forth? Now she'd have to wait until Richard came home and ask him to teach her.

"I'm hopeless," she mourned aloud, stepping back in disgust to glare at the contrary contraption.

Maybe I should pull some weeds. How hard could it be? Decision made, she exited the kitchen to the back porch.

Hesitating on the uneven stoop, she surveyed the garden area, roped off with twine. At her Baltimore home the chef's garden, next to the rear grounds of the estate, maintained regimented rows of herbs and cooking vegetables.

Evelyn ventured closer, unable to identify anything other than a jumble of green interspersed with splashes of color which she assumed were actual edibles. One spot looked worse than the rest.

"I'll start here," she declared.

Grasping a handful of the garden intruders, she yanked so hard, she fell back onto her bottom, landing in a soft pile of dirt. Holding up her fist to inspect the weeds, instead she found a half-dozen stunted carrots.

"Oh, no!" Scrambling to her knees, she attempted to put the dirt encrusted things back in the ground. A sudden stitch in her side made her gasp and she hunched against the pain. Tears of failure blurred her vision.

"Evelyn, are you out here?" Lucinda came through the back door, spotted her on the ground, and took off running toward where she knelt, holding the stupid carrots. "What happened? Are you hurt?" She held out a hand. "Let's get you on your feet, darling."

She offered Richard's aunt a weak smile. "Thank you." Somehow, she managed to keep herself from falling over her own skirts, as Lucinda steadied her.

"What on earth were you trying to do?" She glanced at the sad-looking carrots. "Those are only half grown, not nearly ready to pick."

Her shoulders slumped in defeat. "I thought they were weeds."

"I see." Lucinda tapped a finger to her chin thoughtfully. "You wanted to do a bit of gardening, but you don't know how. Is that it?"

A despairing laugh escaped her. "I don't know how to do anything. I've never performed a single domestic task in my life."

Exasperated, she flung the carrots aside, fighting back useless tears. "Now I am plagued by the thought of meals I cannot prepare, plants that need watering if only I could figure out how to draw water." She sniffed miserably. "Furniture I don't know how to clean."

"Oh, child." Lucinda warmly embraced her. "Rest your head a moment." Obediently Evelyn laid her head on the proffered shoulder. "Our town is filled with women who were once in a similar position. They'd all gladly help you." She raised Evelyn's chin encouragingly. "Why, you'll be a country gal and a proper lawman's wife before you know it."

Halfway to the ranch house, Richard reined in, surprised to see his aunt cantering along on handsome Blue, the stud stallion gifted to her on her last birthday.

"There's a sight for sore eyes," he teased, as their mounts drew abreast and nosed each other in greeting. "What're you doing out here?"

Lucinda flashed a brilliant smile. "I've been visiting your lovely bride. I found her in the garden, pulling what she thought were weeds. Lucky for you I stopped her before she got to all your carrots."

Richard groaned, then chuckled. "Do I have any left in the ground?"

"I stayed for a fast lesson on what not to weed out in a garden. So, you should still have a crop of sorts." Lucinda patted Blue's neck when he danced in place. "This boy wants to run. Good thing I didn't bother with one of those silly sidesaddles." She tightened the reins. "Best get to your wife, and make sure to compliment her on the windows."

"Windows?"

A wide grin wreathed his aunt's lovely face as she sent him a teasing wink. Giving Blue his freedom, the stallion tore away on a fast gallop, Lucinda's melodic laughter floating on the air.

"Well, that wasn't confusing at all," Richard muttered. He snapped Buster's reins to get him moving again.

Minutes later he arrived home, squinting in the afternoon sun toward the aforementioned windows. They did seem to sparkle, with no dust coating the outside.

Not knowing how much housework an expectant mother should be doing, he'd mostly left Evelyn to her own devices, but perhaps learning some of the skills needed to run a home would help her settle in more confidently.

He unsaddled Buster and led him to his stall, filling his bin with oats. Striding toward the back porch, he winced at the damage in the garden where his young carrots had been uprooted. Thankfully his wife hadn't reached the potato plants yet.

"I'm home," he announced, entering the kitchen. "Evelyn?"

"Back here," came the muffled reply. "In the bedroom."

Sounds promising.

He immediately squelched the suggestive thought. As hard as it was to sleep next to her each night without touching her, he'd never pressure a woman into intimacies, not even his wife.

Most assuredly not my wife. When Evelyn was ready to take that step, he'd know.

Removing his hat, he dropped it on the table, following the sounds of thumping and . . . pounding? He rushed into their bedroom in time to see her whacking a nail into one of the walls with the heel of his hobnail boot. "What are you doing?"

She turned, flush-faced, grinning from ear to ear. "I needed a spot to hang my bonnets and such." She nodded toward the bed where a bedraggled hat lay. "I think the brim will smooth out, don't you?"

Richard eyed the pathetic thing, its ribbon half-torn off, its flowers crushed. "I don't think so."

Thinking of how adorable she looked, he moved to her side and reclaimed his boot, setting it on the floor.

Leading her to the bed, he sat her down, removing his bandana to blot her damp forehead. "There's a milliner's in town, right next to the mercantile. Retta Carter's Aunt Millie runs it. A talented lady, makes everything she sells. I'll take you in and you can buy whatever you need."

"Oh, I couldn't," she began.

Richard kissed her, effectively hushing any protest. "Yes, you can," he murmured against her soft lips. He deepened the kiss, delighted when she melted in his arms and kissed him back.

She broke away first, laying her head on his shoulder, snuggling in a way that set his heart to beating fast. "I *would* like a replacement." She poked at the pile of straw next to her. "Thank you, Richard."

He hugged her. "No thanks are needed."

For a moment they sat close together in the room, while a breeze blew in through the open window and fluttered the curtains. Rousing himself from thoughts of what he'd love to do in bed with his new bride— when the time was right—Richard recalled what his aunt had said. "The windows look nice."

She blushed pinker than a rose. "Your Aunt Lucinda spent some time with me today. She helped me with a few things." Pride rang in her voice even as her shoulders sagged. "I, um, ruined some of your carrots. I mistook them for weeds."

"We can plant more." He paused, then decided to tease her a bit. "Did you save those carrots? They'd still be mighty tasty. Sweet. Almost as sweet as you."

The giggle she released as her melancholy fell away warmed his heart. It was up to him to ensure his wife remained safe and happy, a commitment he felt to his very bones.

She straightened, lifting her face to him. "I mentioned to your aunt how I'd like to master some cooking skills. She said several of the women in town would be happy to give me lessons." Earnestness shone in her eyes. "I want to be a good wife, Richard. A real wife. Can you take me to town a few days each week, so I can learn?"

"Of course, whenever you like," he promised.

"Tomorrow?"

"You bet. Tomorrow."

Chapter 8

One week later

Standing near the edge of the Galleria's expansive grounds, Richard looked on as the Pitchford Menagerie Museum and Oddities magically grew from the dust and scrub beneath his feet. "Amazing," he commented.

At his side, Evelyn clutched his arm and nodded. "I confess, I have never seen the like."

When one of the thick tent ropes slid through a worker's grasp and flapped around their heads, she jumped. "My goodness."

Richard winced at the string of foul obscenities the man released, breathing a sigh of relief when the wayward rope was caught and secured. "You didn't hear that," he said to his innocent-eared wife.

"Absolutely did not," she agreed, straight-faced, humor shining in her sky-blue eyes.

Beside her, Knight Gleason bristled like a porcupine. He'd come out to assure the museum workers didn't trample all over Hannah's beloved flowerbeds.

"Well, *ah* heard, an' ah've a mind to knock a few heads togethuh," he muttered. "We got women an' children fixin' to attend. They's no cause fer such profanity." At Richard's amused snort, the Galleria owner's shoulders relaxed. "Ah suppose ah'd cuss some too, if'n ah lost mah grip."

"Gleason, you'd curse as much, if not more." Richard studied the tent as it rose against the bright summer sky. "You ever walk through something like this?"

"Once." Knight puffed on his cigar, considerately blowing the smoke away from Evelyn's sensitive nose. "Ah stayed a few days in Natchez. Had a pocket of poker winnins' beggin' to be spent on wine an' women. Saw a tent goin' up an' paid fer a ticket."

"What did you see, Mister Gleason?" Evelyn asked.

"Why, ah saw a bald man wearin' satin bloomers, swallowin' a sword. Saw a horse prancin' an' high-steppin'. A skinny lil' feller stood on its rump, jugglin' pickaxes. Thought fer sure he'd drop one." He stroked his bearded chin. "Ah recall ladies screamin' in fear when this big ol' elephant—"

At Evelyn's distressed gasp, Knight stopped mid-sentence. He straightened his string tie as he cleared his throat. "Well, ah can't rightly 'member much else."

"Look there." Anxious to redirect his wife's attention, Richard pointed toward a massive cage being lowered to the ground.

Inside, a pair of the largest dogs he'd ever seen lounged on burlap-covered straw, yawning. On the side of the cage a wooden plaque proclaimed in garish letters, THE DANCING DEVIL DOGS.

"I didn't know dogs could dance," he mused.

A loud screech from another wagon had both animals instantly on their feet, bristling fur raised in a stiff ridge down their backs. Deep-throated growls erupted, startling Evelyn. "Oh, my. They can't escape, can they? I was bitten by a large dog when I was a girl."

Richard pried her nails out of his arm and drew her close. "Those bars look strong. They won't get out."

The last thing he wanted was for her to fret about things, especially now. Both Maggie and Aunt Lucinda had warned him of how an expecting woman could be overwhelmed by her emotions. His wife still struggled with the vast differences between the rigid familiarity of Baltimore versus the open wildness of Colorado.

Relieved to feel the tension in her shoulders ease, he guided her toward the back of the Galleria. Knight kept pace as he finished his cigar, pausing to grind it out on the sole of his boot.

Her brows scrunched. "Where are we going?"

"Another cooking lesson," Richard reminded her.

"Oh, I'd almost forgotten." Evelyn brightened. "Missus Lund. She told me to call her Dolores when I met her the other day. She's going to show me how to make a favorite of yours. I understand you're fond of her brown butter cake."

Her sweet thoughtfulness caused his heart to give a hard thump even as his tastebuds rebelled at the thought of eating burned—and badly concocted— baked goods. The last one, a blueberry pie, still seemed to linger on his tongue, and it'd been three days. She'd used salt instead of sugar in the fruit, rendering the dessert inedible.

"I am," he assured her. He appreciated the way she was trying to learn. Recalling how he'd had to choke down her pie with hard-fought enthusiasm . . . it was all he could do to stifle a grimace.

Mary Rush, the Stage House's wonderful cook, baked pies like a dream but chattered worse than any gossip when she had someone new to ear-bend. Her teaching effort had left a lot to be desired. Hopefully Dolores would keep a better eye on Evelyn in the kitchen.

"You know," he began, digging deep for inspiration, "there are places in town we could eat, three times a day. Between the Stage House and the Galleria, we'd never miss a meal."

Approaching the back entrance of the Galleria kitchen, Evelyn dropped her hand from his arm and turned to confront him, disappointment in her gaze and a fierce frown drawing her mouth into a pout.

"You don't like my cooking." The accusation was as flat as the batch of biscuits she'd attempted for last night's supper.

Tread carefully, Blackwood.

He'd found women got touchy over culinary criticism, and his wife was no different. "Not at all. You're learning something new and I'm proud of you."

Her astute gaze held his for a long moment, as if studying him for a lie. Finally, her frown melted, her eyes brightening. "You are? Truly?" She plucked at her skirts, glancing up at him through her lashes. "Even when my biscuits nearly broke your front tooth?"

She looked so hopeful, Richard couldn't resist pulling her in for a hug, mindful of her delicate condition. "Even then."

Behind him, Knight harrumphed, a reminder they weren't alone. "Y'all jes' tickle mah fancy, yessir. Reminds me of them early days with mah lil' dove." He nodded approvingly, straightening the lapels of his waistcoat, brushing off a spot of cigar ash clinging to the expensive fabric. "Ah'm in mah office if'n yew need me."

With a tip of his hat, the burly Galleria owner strode through the rear door, whistling off-key.

Catching Evelyn's elbow, Richard escorted her into the kitchen, removing her shawl in deference to the overly warm room. "Delivered safe and sound, madam." He teasingly dropped a kiss onto the tip of her nose. "I look forward to that cake."

"Can you hurry it up?" Grover Shaw growled at the barber. "I ain't got all day."

There was a little filly over at the whorehouse in Prairie Lick who took real good care of him once a week. Just thinking about her ample curves made his trousers snug, and he reached down to readjust himself.

The bespectacled barber cleared his throat, his lips thinning with obvious annoyance, but he only nodded.

The shop door suddenly crashed open and Floyd barreled inside. "We got trouble, brother." His long strides quickly closed the distance to the barber's chair. "That Jelly fella's been spoutin' off about his silver share being shorted at the smelter."

"Not here," Grover growled, flinging the cutting bowl off his head. He hopped out of the chair and shoved his twin out the door, glancing around to make sure no one was in earshot. "Dumbass! Do you want the damned barber blabbin' to all his customers how we run a dirty business?"

Floyd's face pinched tight, over Grover's anger or pondering the barber indulging in gossip, he wasn't sure. He gave Floyd another shove to help him figure it out. "If that happens, I'll shoot you dead myself."

Not that he would. Unfortunately, the promise he'd made to his ma, to always care for Floyd, still held sway with him. Grover wasn't sure he'd be able to actually shoot his brother despite his ignorant ways.

But Floyd didn't need to know that.

"I-I," Floyd stammered.

Grover slapped him alongside the head. "You what, idjit?"

Floyd audibly gulped. "I'll fix it, I swear."

"See that you do."

Dolores turned the plate around, viewing it from all sides, while Evelyn hid her face and groaned.

"It's not bad, just a bit singed along the edge," the more-than-kind Galleria cook said. "We can cut that off before we add the butter sauce."

"Except I burned the sauce." Evelyn peeked through her fingers toward the stove where a pot still smoldered. "I swear, I thought I had everything in hand."

Her throat thickened with emotion. Never had she dreamed such a domestic task as cooking would be her undoing. "I'm a failure."

"Now, now, don't fret." Dolores rubbed her shoulder. "It takes time to learn your way around a kitchen. I believe you'll fare just fine, child. Give yourself more credit for even wanting to learn."

"But that's just it. I don't know if I *do* want to learn." She blotted her perspiring face on her apron. The air in the kitchen stifled her, though all the windows were open. Her back ached, her fingers were wrinkly from continually dunking them in water to wash off various substances she'd already spilled, and she didn't want to think about what her clumsiness had cost Mister Gleason in wasted foodstuffs.

She met Dolores's compassionate expression as a feeling of overwhelming ineptitude welled up inside her. "This life is foreign to me. Each day I'm challenged anew with something I swear is destined to make me flounder. If I can't manage a cake or a blasted pan of biscuits, how am I ever going to deal with a husband and child?"

Evelyn tugged on her apron but couldn't dislodge the knot tied in the back. Exhaling in frustration, she sagged against the counter and stared at her pathetic offering. "I'm hopeless," she bemoaned.

A stern, yet quavering voice drifted in from the doorway leading out to the hall connecting the Galleria's salons. "Stop moping, right this instant."

She spun, gaping at Richard's grandmother. Leaning on her cane and dressed in widow's weeds as usual, she dominated the vast kitchen as if it were a mere closet. "Missus, er, Granny Nia, what are you doing here?"

"I came with Lucinda on her visit to Mister Gleason's wife and son." Nia advanced, cane tapping on the wooden floor. "Made my howdy-dos and decided to look for something stronger than tea." She paused at the counter where the charred baking lesson sat. Sniffing the air, she sent a withered glance over her shoulder, spying the pot of ruined sauce.

Turning back to Evelyn, she lifted one silver brow. "Well, missy. What have you to say for yourself?"

Inadequacies towering over Evelyn like an unscalable mountain, she burst into tears.

The old woman was instantly at her side, moving faster than one would think her capable of, enveloping her in a warm, one-armed embrace. Granny Nia's bergamot pomade tickled her nose as the seconds ticked by.

Finally, Evelyn managed to get herself under control. With one last sniffle, she lifted her head. "I'm sorry, I don't know why I'm so weepy."

Granny Nia snickered. "Lord, when I was carrying my boys, it seemed all I did was blubber." Releasing Evelyn, she eyed her and briskly said, "Now that you've got it out of your system, there'll be no more nonsense about being hopeless. Understand?"

"Yes, ma'am." She stood taller under that piercing stare.

Fumbling in her pocket, the elder lady produced a handkerchief. "Blow your nose."

As Evelyn obeyed the curt demand, Dolores winked. "I'll just leave you in Missus Blackwood's capable hands while I tend to my daughter's lunch. I'm sure she's still out in the stables with the horses." The cook bustled from the kitchen.

"Sit." Granny Nia pointed to the nearest chair. "You look near ready to keel over." Taking a seat across from her, the old woman balanced the cane across her knees, her eyes never leaving Evelyn's. Time stretched from one minute into two, until she stated bluntly, "I almost killed my husband."

"W-What?" Evelyn blinked, wondering if she needed to clean her ears out. She couldn't have heard what she thought she heard.

The merest smile flitted across Granny Nia's lips. "Yes, indeed. Early in our marriage, August became a keen fisherman. Used to tromp the banks of the Patapsco regularly." She shuddered. "I hate fish. Smelly, slimy things. My man would spend hours trolling that river and pull in striped bass, bring them home on a hank of twine, and expect me to clean and cook them. The first time, he caught six. When he proudly dropped them at my feet, I ran screeching out the kitchen door."

Nia's expression, half horror, half humor, drew a giggle from Evelyn. "But you did cook them," she guessed, relaxing under that soft, raspy voice.

"Yes, eventually. I recall the stink of them from laying on the floor all night long because I refused to touch them, and August was stubborn about what he considered women's work. I finally gave in the next morning. Took them outside to clean. August ate half of them, complained of stomach ills an hour later, and spent the next day and a half vomiting into the privy. I didn't know fish needed to be gutted and cleaned immediately. I could have poisoned the man."

She eyed Evelyn shrewdly. "Once or twice over the years I was sorely tempted to let the fish rot on the floor. I loved my husband, but he tried my patience to the bitter edge of sanity."

"Did you ever cook fish again?"

The Blackwood matriarch drew herself up proudly. "I make the best poached bass in Baltimore." She nudged the plate containing the sad looking cake. "If I can learn to master a despised fishy thing, you can certainly achieve success in baking my grandson's favorite dessert." She cupped Evelyn's cheek. "I have faith in you, girl."

With her bruised spirit restored, she covered the chilled, gnarled fingers. "Will you help me, Granny Nia?"

Those faded brown eyes softened. "Of course I will."

"And if I need advice with child-rearing?" Her voice wobbled slightly. "I think about it all the time. Lucinda has already told me worrying isn't good for the babe."

"Much of that will come naturally, my dear. The rest"—Nia shrugged—"you'll learn. Plenty of ladies around here will offer advice, I'm sure."

Rising stiffly to her feet, she hobbled toward the stove. "Now, let's toss out this scorched sauce and start over."

Leaning back in his chair, Richard patted his belly. He'd eaten two helpings of Dolores's excellent braised beef tongue and turnips, finishing off the hearty meal with a large slice of the cake Evelyn had made under the cook's tutelage.

"I might have to loosen my buttons," he groaned, flashing a grin at his bride who fidgeted in her seat next to him. "Which could cause a scandal in here, seeing as there are unmarried ladies about."

He nodded toward Clem Washburn and his family, tucked into a corner of the Galleria dining salon, his daughters chattering happily while the younger boys tried to glare intimidatingly at the cowpokes and gamblers charmed by their sisters' pretty display.

Evelyn dabbed her mouth with her napkin. "I heard the next-to-oldest, John, I believe, will be coming home next year. Nellie Washburn told me the Carter brothers paid for university fees, and their eldest son has already returned." Her expression held a look of wonderment. "The kindness in this town is humbling."

"I fully agree." Richard pushed back his chair, holding his breath while the delicious food in his stomach settled. Rising, he offered an elbow. "It's a fine night. Care to take a turn through town with me, Missus Blackwood?"

"I'd be delighted."

Outside, the evening held a decent breeze. They strolled silently at first, waving to others who'd had the same idea of enjoying the beautiful early-summer night. Behind them, Pitchford's tents rose in a dark smudge against the cleared area on Galleria grounds.

"The Menagerie Museum opens tomorrow." Richard eased Evelyn around a cracked board, pausing to let a trio of rambunctious children rush by. "I understand a parade is scheduled. Would you feel up to attending?"

She nodded, her golden curls bouncing. "I would, very much." Excitement shone from her eyes. "Lucinda and Dub are going too. It should be fun."

The easy way in which she willingly embraced his family warmed his heart. He'd also taken note of how she'd bent an ear toward his granny, who'd briefly sat with them during the first course of their meal at the Galleria. She'd fussed over the texture of the turnips Dolores had served, but that didn't stop her from indulging in an extra serving. Granny had left before dessert, winking at Evelyn as she rose with the help of her cane and his supporting arm.

"You know, your cake was especially fine," he began.

She waved away his praise. "Thank your grandmother. I scorched the sauce and just about set it all on fire. I was ready to cry into my apron in defeat when she came into the kitchen, told me to buck up, and showed me how to cook the sauce without burning it."

In the lamplight glow, her eyes shone as bright as the stars above. A strong wave of affection toward her entwined itself with the desire that always seemed to be present.

"She's wonderful, Richard. All your family is."

"Does that include me?" Though blatantly fishing for a compliment, he passed it off as a jest but found himself anticipating her answer as she faced him on the quiet street.

As good as things seemed to be going in their marriage, he still worried she'd come to regret it. Living in a small mining town was a far cry from high society life back East.

A lovely pink stained her cheeks. "I-I have always found you most kind—"

A panicked shout from across the road interrupted the moment.

Chapter 9

"Barbershop's on fire!"

The older gentleman she recalled seeing when she'd first arrived in town rushed past, heading toward a squat building where dark plumes of smoke reached into the night sky.

"Evie, stay on the boardwalk." Richard sprinted toward the burning building, hollering, "Hank, stop! Don't open the door."

Lifting her skirts, Evelyn crossed the road, standing back a good distance from the smoky area, wanting to help in any way she could if needed.

Richard gripped Hank's shoulder. "We don't want to make the fire worse. Fetch Ben. I've got to see if anyone else is inside."

Hank nodded and hurried toward the jail.

Richard cast her a warning glance. "Keep back," he cautioned, before darting around the side of the building.

Her heart pounded a rapid beat in her throat. Fear for her new husband brought into clear focus the undeniable truth of how much he meant to her.

Not only did she need Richard in her life because he'd fathered her child, but because she cared deeply for him.

Gently rubbing her stomach where their babe slumbered, she prayed, "Lord, please keep him safe."

Shouts filled the air, the dusty street seething with activity as men joined the rescue while women crowded the sidewalks. She recognized Sheriff Lang's other deputy carrying a bucket and barking orders. He began scooping water from a nearby horse trough, boasting its own well supply. More help arrived, some with buckets of their own, as they formed a line to the barbershop.

While Hank steadily pumped well water, the makeshift fire brigade passed filled buckets down the line to throw onto the fire, now visible through the wooden planks of the front walls.

Lucinda came alongside her. "Evelyn, are you all right?" She quickly took in the scene. "Where's Richard?"

Evelyn's attention remained riveted on the burning barbershop, waiting for Richard to reappear. "He went to see if anyone was inside."

Her voice cracked on the last word, as his aunt wrapped a comforting arm around her shoulders.

Together they watched the men tossing bucket after bucket of water on the structure in an attempt to douse the fire, somehow managing to keep the blaze from spreading to nearby shops.

Lucinda's grip tightened. "Did Richard go inside?"

"I-I don't know, he ran around to the back."

"Most of these shops contain storage rooms. I believe Henry Tipple lives in his. Richard must have gone looking for him."

"What's taking him so long?" Evelyn gnawed her thumbnail ragged as panic rose up inside her.

"Look." Lucinda pointed toward the building. "He's safe."

Spotting Richard rounding the building, she released a sigh of relief. Coated in ash, he otherwise appeared no worse for wear, carrying a limp form over his shoulder. Two others ran over to help him lower the man to the ground, who appeared to be dazed.

"Jack Jaworski," Lucinda murmured, frowning.

"Who?"

"He's the smithy." Worry deepened her tone. "What about Henry?"

"Let me through, ladies," a gruff voice demanded from behind them.

Evelyn hastily stepped aside as Doc Sheaton strode to the injured man and knelt, opening the medical bag he carried.

"There's a nasty cut, Jack." He produced a square of cotton, stanching the blood from the smithy's brow. "Any sharp pains?"

"No," came the muffled reply.

Moments later, with support from Richard and the doctor, the smithy stood on somewhat unsteady feet. "I'm fine," he insisted, then wobbled alarmingly. "I ain't got time for this."

"You're coming back to the office so I can examine you further, without all these interfering ladies around," Sheaton said firmly, sending a wink toward Evelyn and Lucinda.

"No, I'm not—"

"Unless you'd like me to strip you down right here on the street, you most certainly are."

Richard squeezed Jack's shoulder. "Go with the doc, we'll take care of everything."

The two men exchanged grim looks, but the smithy reluctantly gave in. "All right," he grumbled. Waving off additional assistance, he followed the doctor back to his office.

Meeting Evelyn's regard, Richard mouthed, "I'll be back," before joining the others to extinguish the blaze. The next half hour seemed to last an eternity, until the damaged but still standing building was brought under control to the loud cheers of the townsfolk who'd gathered to help.

Expecting Richard to join her, Evelyn was surprised to see him motion to the deputy and a few other men. Silently they hurried to the back of the building again.

"That's not good," Lucinda said sadly.

Evelyn swallowed hard, worry for a man she'd never met gripping her heart.

For endless minutes, the entire town seemed to hold its breath.

Finally, Richard reappeared, grimy and sweaty, alongside the equally soot-blackened deputy.

Between them they carried a badly-burned man who could only be Henry Tipple.

Richard took a seat across from Jack Jaworski. "Tell me again what happened."

Finding both Jack and Henry inside the barber's quarters, the room already in flames, had shaken Richard to the core. Henry was beyond help but Jaworski was only unconscious, reinforcing the tough choice to pull the smithy to safety from the fire's stifling smoke first before it overcame everything in its path.

It took over an hour to extinguish the blaze enough for them to get inside and retrieve Henry Tipple's body. Doc reckoned the old man died not because of the burns on his body but was instead severely incapacitated by a crushing blow to the back of his skull, allowing the smoke to invade his lungs.

Jack returned Richard's gaze steadily. Reddened scrapes dotted the smithy's face and hands, his hair badly singed, bandages peeking through his torn, tattered clothing where the doc had tended to various injuries.

"It's like I said, Deputy. I closed up early and went next door for a trim. Soon as I sat down, Henry excused himself to go into the back for a bowl. I told him he didn't need a danged bowl to cut my hair, but you know how Henry was."

Sadness shadowed Jack's face. "He hadn't been gone long when I heard this crash. I figured he'd dropped something. By the time I realized it was more than that and went to check on him, smoke was drifting from under the door to his living quarters."

His jaw clenched, and he took a deep breath. "When I tried to open the door, it was locked. I had to kick it in."

"It was locked?" Richard grunted. "Why would he lock the door?"

Lips pinched tight, Jack shook his head. "I wondered the same thing, then I spotted him on the floor by a wall of cabinets near the back. I ran over to pick him up with the intention of getting us both the hell out of there." He shrugged. "That's the last I remember until you arrived and hefted me over your shoulder like a seed bag."

"A beam from the ceiling came down and pinned you both."

Richard pushed away from the desk and stood, needing to pace.

If the blow hadn't been caused by falling ceiling timber, had someone murdered the quiet, unassuming man? It made no sense at all. Henry Tipple had no enemies or scandals that'd cause someone to want him dead, at least nothing Richard was aware of.

He returned to his chair, the evening's events churning through his weary brain. "Anything out of the ordinary happen while you were getting your trim?"

"Come to think of it, Henry did make a peculiar comment about the Shaw brothers."

"Yeah?"

Jack nodded. "Evidently Grover came in for a haircut, oh, maybe a couple hours before Henry usually closed up for the evening. Halfway through his brother ran inside and said something about 'that Jelly fella' asking questions about his silver share being off at the smelting company."

"Jelly?"

Jack grinned wryly. "That'd be Stewart Perth, one of the newer miners near Rocky Gulch. His lady love calls him Jelly because of his fondness for her homemade jam, and it sort of stuck." He scratched his chin thoughtfully. "Grover was none too happy, it seemed. Jumped out of the chair angrier than a ragin' bull. He ripped the bowl off his head and threw it across the room. Put a big dent in the side when it hit the wall. Then he grabbed Floyd by the neck and dragged him out the door."

Richard's mind was already filling in some suspicious blanks. "What else?"

"Henry was steamed, said Grover never came back to get his hair evened up. Didn't pay, either."

"And Henry complained to the next customer, who happened to be you."

"Yep."

"Anything more?"

He shook his head. "All that comes to mind."

"Thanks, Jack. You're free to go. I might need you to speak to Sheriff Lang, once he gets back into town. Supposed to be heading in from a fishing trip sometime tomorrow."

"I can do that." Jack came to his feet, a grimace of pain crossing his face. "You think those Shaw fellas had something to do with Henry's death?"

Furious one of Little Creede's citizens could have been murdered under his watch, Richard growled, "Don't know. But I'm sure as hell gonna find out."

Chapter 10

Standing in the lobby of the Galleria, Richard mulled over the barbershop fire.

Joshua had returned early this morning from his fishing trip. Richard planned on meeting with him in a few hours.

He rubbed wearily at his eyes. *First, I need more coffee.*

The Galleria kitchen always kept a full pot on the enormous cookstove Dolores Lund so easily managed. Yawning, Richard entered the kitchen, surprised to see her bent over the sink, sniffling into her apron. Alarmed, he swiftly crossed to her side. "What's wrong?"

"Oh, Richard, I'm in such a mess." Wiping at her wet cheeks, Dolores allowed him to lead her to the table, sinking into the chair he held out. "I must calm myself before Luellen wakes and comes down for her breakfast."

"Why don't you start by telling me what pains you so. Is it your health? Did one of the horses sicken?" He knew Dolores and her daughter Luellen highly prized their palominos, breeding the beautiful animals in the Galleria stables and selling them to a very select clientele from as far away as Sulphur Hills. He'd already made plans to purchase a gentle mare for Evelyn, as soon as their babe was born and she ended her confinement.

Dolores retrieved a handkerchief from her pocket and blew her nose. "No, nothing like that. I was served notice last night from the smelter, saying I'm short on the ore Sweeney's claim pulls in for me. I'd asked for an advance based on my usual tally, which I have done in the past when bills came due and money was tight. Never a problem, either. Everyone knows the claim is good for it."

She wiped at fresh tears. "Bless his everlasting heart, Sweeney set us up wisely, almost as if he'd known he would not be around in our twilight years."

Sweeney Lund had died a few years back in an explosion at the Carter mines. Richard had helped pull wounded miners from the rubble, a grievous task he'd never forget. The Carters had made sure all mine claims had remained in effect for the survivors of the tragedy and their family members.

He steadied Dolores's trembling frame. "Why didn't you just ask Knight for the advance? He'd have given it gladly."

"Oh, I couldn't impose. The man has done enough for me, what with letting me use the stables for my breeders and never asking for a penny in rent."

Richard grunted in understanding. Gleason's generosity was legendary in Little Creede. "Still, your claim should continuously produce the same amount of ore, and the net worth wouldn't fluctuate much, if at all. Maybe it's a ledger error, something easy to straighten out."

"I don't know," she replied fretfully. "I suppose I should have paid better attention. But all this time I've never had a speck of trouble with the claim. The ore is pulled, sent off with all the others, and the payment comes here, regular as rain."

Her normally cheerful countenance crinkled into lines of worry. "And I trust Mister Heath, of course."

"Dolores, Mister Heath no longer owns the smelter."

Granted, the man had been fair-minded and decent. His only fault—a desperate gambling problem—became his downfall.

Her brows drew into a deep frown. "What?"

"I thought you knew. He lost it, um, he had to sell out." Richard hated adding to the woman's burden, but he wouldn't lie to her, either. "Two gents, name of Shaw, own it now. Brothers. I don't know a lot about them except they might be, er, not fully honest."

"Have I been swindled?" Her voice squeaked alarmingly as she jumped to her feet. "We have to let the others know. Thank the Lord I've got the horses. But goodness, that monthly disbursement is all the mining families have to live on! If we're being cheated, something has to be done."

"Something will. Soon as I notify the sheriff, then saddle up and grab me a deputy," Richard promised.

"What d'ya think we'll find?" Ben Parsons asked, as he guided his stallion over a clot of rocks embedded in the trail.

"Hell if I know. Stay alert, though. I still think these two had something to do with Henry's death." Richard let Cloud, his young draft mare, have her lead when she strained at the bit. His main mount, Buster was currently on loan to his brother while Robert's mare was in season and wouldn't be returned until they knew for certain she was in foaling.

They'd started out early, determined to uncover what kind of trouble the Shaws were causing their ore clientele since they'd taken over, nine months earlier. With only one facility in the region, it was nigh-on impossible to keep things honest and not act like a monopoly.

Nobody had cause to suspect nefarious goings-on. The Shaws, for all their repulsiveness, seemed to be making a proper go of collecting raw ore from the Carter and Rocky Gulch mines, rendering it into bullion bars, and sending them to Georgetown for final processing. Until yesterday, Richard hadn't a clue the profit back to the miners might suffer an undercut. Or if they would come under fire for shorting their own claims.

Doubtful any of this stems from Georgetown. Which left the Shaw's business tactics as a probable culprit.

As expected, Joshua had been infuriated at the latest heinous goings-on; the fire and then, the suspicions of crooked practices out at the smelter. He'd been striding toward the blacksmith forge to speak with Jack Jaworski when Richard nabbed Ben as backup for the trip out to confront the Shaws.

The longer, narrower path to the facility came into view, and Ben cursed as Lucky caught a hoof on a protruding rock. "This is ridiculous. Heath kept this road clear for the mules and carts."

"Agreed." Richard slowed as the side of the building revealed overgrown, dried-out grasses close to the outer walls where escaping heat and embers from the blast furnace could provoke a brush fire. He scowled, pointing to a section of brown scrub. "If it catches a spark, there'll be hell to pay."

Ben nodded, his lips tightening as he took in the condition of the smelter. Several ore carts had been emptied and abandoned, one sporting a broken wheel. "Idiots, for sure."

Dismounting, they ground-tethered their horses in a spot of shade. Richard motioned Ben around one side of the gaping entrance while he slipped past the other, both hands hovering over his holster.

Inside the stifling interior, he bit back a snarl at the unorganized mess. Men, stripped to their trousers, hurried between the roaster and the blast furnace, their torsos dark from soot and sweat. Mules brayed, unaccustomed to the miserable heat inside, their hooves clopping over the rough ground as they shifted against the bracketing hitches of the carts immobilizing their slumped bodies.

"Jesus Lord." Ben grabbed the arm of a worker as he dashed past. "Get these animals out of here," he shouted above the roar of the furnace. "What the hell's wrong with you people?"

"You ain't my boss," the man snarled, but backed off when Ben flashed his badge. Muttering under his breath, the worker snagged two others to help. Silently the trio unhitched the mules and dragged them toward the opening.

"And give them some water," Ben ordered. He removed his bandana from around his neck and mopped his forehead. "Blasted fools."

"Yeah." Richard strode to the side of the furnace room where Homer Heath used to keep a small office. "I'd say the Shaw boys have some things to answer for, starting with Dolores's shorted claim."

Not bothering to knock, he burst through the door with Ben close behind.

Floyd spat a clump of chaw on the office floorboards as he stomped toward the door where Blackwood and that other deputy had just departed.

Grover fisted the jackass's suspenders and jerked him back. "Calm down, dammit."

"Leggo." His brother swung a fist wildly. "They got no right to question us. If you ain't got the guts to kill the law, I sure as hell do."

Shoving hard, Grover forced him onto a chair. "They got nothin' on us, y'hear? Not a thing as long as you keep your mouth shut and your gun holstered. Some biddy wants to moan and groan over her claim, so what? 'Bout all the law did was give us grief when they saw the mules."

Floyd sprang to his feet in a face-off. "If we was back in Chicago we'd be takin' care of the law with bullets."

"We ain't in Chicago, stupid. We can't do anything where there's witnesses. Ain't we already suspects in that fire, thanks to you?" Longing to plow a fist in his stubborn brother's face, Grover paced around the stifling office, thinking furiously.

He'd promised his mother—on her deathbed and gasping for breath against the consumption destroying her lungs—he'd take care of his twin, younger by ten minutes, who'd proven himself dumber than dirt at a young age.

Despite Floyd's determination over the years to pick fights, shoot first, do everything in his power to land them both in jail, Grover'd made good on his promise. Getting out of Illinois was the only way to keep them alive.

Now, when they'd finally started making money, using what they'd learned as part of the Pines organization in Chicago's seedy underbelly, the hothead's idiocy threatened to blow it all to hell.

"They can't tie the old man's death to us," Floyd blustered. "We ain't left no witnesses."

"The smithy's still alive. Weren't you listenin'? He spilled his guts enough to have Blackwood comin' out here to nose around. Askin' questions. Just because he left with a warnin' over the stinkin' mules, don't mean he's not watchin'. Trouble'll come back on us if we're not careful."

Grover stalked over to the trough where the bullion bars cooled, and stuck his head under the pump, until the water eased his urge to pound his brother bloody.

One of us needs to keep their wits and as usual, it falls to me.

Straightening, he slicked back his wet hair. "We'll lay low for a few days afore we head into town and fix things."

The late-afternoon sun cast shadows over the tents erected on Galleria grounds. A wafting breeze kept flies and mosquitoes away, something Evelyn was thankful for. Grasping her husband's arm, they strolled through the Menagerie gates.

She tilted her sunbonnet brim to protect her eyes, as he paid Pitchford's entry fee of a half-dime per person.

"Looks like the entire town is here," she commented, waving to Betsey Loman who manned a pie booth. She'd met the hardworking merchant when she'd visited the Loman's store in search of embroidery thread. The woman's champion baked goods were sure to sell out quickly.

Next to her, Silas Loman tipped his hat to the ladies with one hand and collected coins in the other.

"I hope she makes a decent profit." Richard guided her around a pack of screeching boys. "Don't let go of my arm."

"I won't." It was endearing the way her husband adjusted his gait to allow for her shorter stride. With so much to see, she didn't want to miss anything. Quite a few of the men escorted wives and children, some looking less than thrilled to be assigned such a chore. Uncle Dub had mentioned a makeshift sharpshooting area that was sure to be popular once the menfolk had done their family duty.

She pointed to a tent where loud whoops could be heard. "Can we go in?"

THE DANCING DEVIL DOGS canvas sign propped near the entrance proclaimed what was happening inside. Though the sheer size of the beasts and growling rumbles had startled her the other day, her curiosity was piqued.

"Sure can." Richard steered her toward the open tent flap.

His aunt's holler caught their attention. "Richard, your granny needs you." They paused, turning as she hurried in their direction. "Stubborn woman insists on walking back to the Stage House," she added, a frown marring her usually lovely face.

"Where is she?" Evelyn asked, a touch of amusement lingering over Nia's orneriness.

"I sat her down at the pie stand. Betsey's got her talking about favorite crust recipes, but that diversion won't last." Lucinda blew out a frazzled breath. "Mister Gleason grabbed Dub for some vague reason right before I noticed how weary Mother Nia looked. Now I can't find him. But she'll listen to you, Richard."

"I'll deal with it. Hell, I'll carry her back to the Stage House if need be." He dropped a kiss onto Evelyn's forehead. "I won't be gone long." With a brief squeeze to his aunt's shoulder, he headed toward the Lomans' stand.

"I'm sorry I had to interrupt your fun." Lucinda edged her off the path. "Let's find you a spot of shade."

"I'm fine," Evelyn protested, but let herself be guided beneath a flowering hawthorn. She leaned on the trunk and wiped the perspiration from her temples. "Guess I didn't realize how warm it's gotten."

Lucinda eyed her critically. "Your cheeks are red. Why don't I fetch you a beverage? My grandchildren set up a lemonade stand near the juggler exhibition. I'll swipe a tumbler of something refreshing for both of us."

"Thank you, I am a bit parched."

Back at the Stage House, Granny was in rare form. "Stop hovering," she ordered.

"Drink your water and I'll think about it." Richard waited, tapping one foot, until she sighed gustily.

"Water has no taste." But she lifted the glass to her lips for a deep drink. "Satisfied?"

"Pretty much." He bent over the back of her chair and smacked a kiss to one lined cheek.

"Get away and let me enjoy my meal." The gruffness in her voice was at odds with the soft pat she placed on his chin, all she could reach of him.

"You look especially hale and hearty today." He longed to tell her how much he adored her, but if he said anything else she'd probably whack him for being too sentimental.

"Hmph." She eyed him as she cut into her poached pears and sugared huckleberries. "I'm not susceptible to such folderol, my boy." She crammed a loaded fork into her mouth, chewing slowly, swallowing with evident enjoyment. "This is quite fine. Too bad I only have the one serving."

Beside her, Dub slapped his leg and hooted. "Ma, you never disappoint."

He'd ordered up several favorites for her, grunting in approval when she ignored her baked pork belly in favor of indulging in dessert. Richard didn't care what she ate first as long as she cleaned each plate.

Aunt Lucinda had been exactly right, Granny hadn't looked well, though food and rest had started to renew the color in her cheeks, easing Richard's worry. Underneath all that bluster and grit lay a proud woman in the twilight of her years.

She'd box my ears if I ever treated her like an old lady.

He set his hat on his head. "I'm going back to the menagerie. Mind yourself." He paused, touching its brim in teasing tribute. "Young lady."

Richard exited to the sound of Granny's infectious cackles.

With Lucinda gone, Evelyn straightened and glanced around at the tents, some empty and silent. Others contained applause and excited chatter.

Impatient for Richard to return so they could continue enjoying the entertainment together, she meandered toward a few clustered tents, curious to discover what they held. One stood apart from the others, its flap pulled back but the interior dark.

Curiosity propelled her feet forward. Surely it wouldn't hurt to peek inside. A brightly painted sign tacked over the doorframe read, *Madame Zoee. Fortune-Teller and Mystic.*

Her heartbeat quickened with excitement. She'd heard of gypsy palm readers, never thinking she'd get a chance to actually meet one. Back East, such otherworldly things were frowned upon as lower-class entertainment.

Venturing closer, Evelyn noted the tent flap was partially open, loosely secured back with a piece of rope. Squinting inside, her eyes slowly adjusted to the shadowy interior. A beam of dappled sun behind her provided illumination over a round table set with three chairs and draped in crimson fabric. Nearby, a wrought iron floor candelabra held several crooked candles.

A round glass ball rested on a wooden stand in the center of the table, and what she guessed to be tarot cards were splayed out, face down, in front of the high-backed chair located directly across from the other two, smaller ones.

Inching inside, she studied the interior, fascinated by the sense of mystery the sparse decorations induced. Moving to the center of the small space, she circled, noting how the dimness offered by the thick fabric of the walls added a strange sense of doom to the overall effect.

By design, of course, she thought. Even the air contained an unfamiliar, uncomfortable odor that caused her to sneeze.

"Ugh," she muttered, wiping her nose as she debated the wisdom of returning to the tent later to see Madame Zoee's exhibition.

A swooshing noise, followed by almost complete darkness, sent unease jolting through her. She spun toward the exit.

Two shadowy figures barred her escape. Only a thread of light peeked inside from the closed tent flap.

Evelyn gasped, panicked.

Backing away from the threatening presences, she bumped into the candelabra, sending the candles crashing to the ground.

The menacing hiss of, "Shut up, or you're gonna get hurt," froze the scream bubbling up in her throat.

Chapter 11

Exiting the Stage House, Richard put aside thoughts of his contrary grandmother for now, picking up his pace, eager to get back to his new bride. He'd been a perfect gentleman so far, giving her some time to adjust to their marriage even as the need to touch her, lie with her again, grew stronger each passing day.

She was as beautiful and sweet as he remembered from their time together back East, reinforcing the reason he'd proposed to her in the first place. Despite what she presumed, it hadn't *only* been because he felt duty bound to do the right thing by her. He'd cared for her deeply then, and he cared even more now. Knowing she carried his child filled him with overwhelming protectiveness.

Mine.

Granny had once assured him—and Robert— they'd both find love. It had happened for his brother. Richard was determined to embrace his chance at love too.

Entering the grounds to the menagerie, he headed toward the spot he'd left her. Halfway there, he spied his aunt striding toward him, a look of distress on her face.

Worry rose inside him as he strode to her side. "What is it?" He peered over her shoulder, but his wife was nowhere to be seen. "Where's Evelyn?"

Lucinda twisted her hands together. "I can't find her."

Knots formed in his gut. "What do you mean, you can't find her?"

"She seemed pale, so I left her under a shade tree while I went to fetch some water. When I came back, she was gone." Anxiety, mingled with a good dose of fear, shone in her eyes. "I searched the grounds but didn't see her anywhere."

"Show me where you left her."

His aunt spun around. "This way." They quickly overtook the slower meandering of the fair-sized crowd, stopping near a bushy tree alongside a row of tents. "I was only gone ten minutes," she said worriedly.

Frowning, Richard studied the area. His first inclination leaned toward Evelyn wandering off to see some sights, perhaps even poke into a few of the tents. Spotting Harrison Carter enjoying a family picnic under a large willow near the food stand, he walked over to them. "Have any of you seen Evelyn?"

"Not lately." Harrison leaned in to say something to his wife, rising as Retta waved before turning her attention back to her brood. "Misplaced that pretty new bride of yours already, Blackwood?" he drawled.

"Seems so." Richard fought to tamp down his unease. "I'd appreciate an assist in locating her."

Harrison clapped his shoulder reassuringly. "She's got to be somewhere close. We'll find her."

Evelyn quivered in fright as the two ruffians advanced. Only when they stopped, mere inches from her, was she able to make out their features. In the dim lighting they looked vaguely familiar, one of them scarred over part of his face.

"Ain't you Blackwood's woman?" the unscarred man asked, a sneer curling his lips.

Gulping down her terror, all she could do was nod in answer to his question. Her hands rose to her middle in a mother's instinct to protect her child. Did they mean to hurt her? Were they part of the menagerie, angry because she'd stumbled into their tent without permission?

She hoped for the latter, so she could offer up an apology and leave.

The scarred one edged closer and she jerked back, stumbling over a fallen candle. His hand shot out and grabbed her elbow, tugging her up against his body.

His hard stare pinned her, the grip on her arm painful. "It ain't safe for him to leave you alone like this. Anythin' could happen."

The stench of tobacco and whiskey on his breath made her stomach churn sickeningly. Her legs trembling beneath her, a lie rolled off her lips. "My-my husband will be back any minute now. He only left to-to get me a glass of juice."

She eased away, putting some distance between them, but he didn't release her arm.

The other one spoke, pure disdain coating his tone. "Heard you was from back East." He crowded up next to her, his beady eyes locked on her breasts. "Things is dangerous out here, little lady. A beautiful woman like you could get into all sorts of trouble."

Evelyn shuddered. There was no missing the threat in his voice.

Twisting her arm from the scarred man's grasp, she retreated until the wall of the tent stopped her. Her mind worked furiously on a way to escape.

If I scream will they hurt me? Could she somehow talk her way out of this situation?

Suddenly, outside light filled the tent as a large-boned woman swept inside. Dressed in a bright blue dress with an array of fringed satin shawls haphazardly draped over her wide rounded shoulders, she took in the scene with eyes as dark as night.

Tossing black, wildly curling hair away from a lined, surprisingly attractive face, she slammed long-fingered hands on her voluminous hips, scowling at both men.

"What you think you're doing, eh?" Shifting that sharp gaze to Evelyn, her expression softened. "Are you all right, *bebe*?"

The scar-faced man shot her a mean look. "Leave now, lady."

The woman scoffed, "The name is Madame Zoee, and this is my tent, you ugly *porcine*." With a glance over her shoulder, she called out, "Harvey, *viens ici*!" She bared her teeth. "I think you are the ones who leave."

Before anyone could respond, a huge, brawny man, clothed in only a tight-fitting pair of britches, entered the tent. The muted afternoon light behind him reflected off his bald head and outlined his thick muscles in stark detail.

"What is it, sweetling?" Black brows drawing down into a deep V, he glowered at the intruders blocking Evelyn's escape. "Are these two bothering you, miss?"

"*Cheri,* there you are." Madame Zoee batted outrageously long lashes at him as she gestured toward Evelyn's tormentors. "*S'il vous plait*, take out the trash?"

Harvey clenched his fists until his impressive biceps bulged. "You heard the lady. Git!"

Time stood still for a long moment, before the scarred man flicked her a hateful glare and muttered, "Better tell your man to be more careful, or you might get hurt."

With that bold statement he strode toward the exit, trailed by the other one. Never taking his eyes off either, Harvey stomped behind them, remaining on their heels the entire way.

Weak and lightheaded, Evelyn fought for breath, unable to get enough air. Her legs shook beneath her as Madame Zoee hurried her way, calling to her. Even though she saw the woman's lips move, recognized the concern on her face, it was as if her mind no longer worked.

She reached for the table to steady herself as darkness crept into the edges of her vision and the world spun around her.

Lucinda's distressed gaze encompassed Richard and Harrison. "Should I go get Dub?"

"Naw, I'm sure Evelyn's nearby," Richard replied hastily, unwilling for his aunt to feel additional guilt.

"Ma," Harrison said gently, "why don't you stay with Retta and the young'uns for a bit while I help the deputy locate his wayward wife?"

With a faint smile, Lucinda hastened to join her grandchildren and Retta.

"Appreciate this, Harrison." Richard pointed toward the north. "If you start at that end, we'll meet in the middle."

"Right."

Toward the south, the afternoon breeze had cooled, an indication it'd be dusk soon. Richard kept a sharp eye on the rougher paths where many feet had already flattened the grass. Along the open areas, food stalls remained, some flush with assorted delicacies and others emptied and ready to be packed up for the day.

Shouts, from children and parents alike, poured out of various tents, so he headed in that direction. If Evelyn had succumbed to the temptation of a tent show, he'd feel a bit of relief since chairs had been set inside each one for the ladies' comfort.

Straightening his hat, he marched up to the nearest tent and peered inside the flap, blinking at the sight of a marionette show, two dolls dressed as pirates bowing and posing on a makeshift stage while a puppeteer worked their strings. A ring of children sat on the ground, enraptured.

Not seeing Evelyn along the small crowd of adults standing behind the children, he retreated and strode to the next tent, finding it empty. Frustrated, growing more worried, he searched for anything that might've fascinated a lone, curious woman.

The dog tent perhaps, except its flap was tied shut, a crudely lettered sign pinned to the canvas indicating the animals and their handler had left for the day.

Ready to stand in the middle of the Menagerie and shout his wife's name like a madman, he spied a smaller, yet gaudy tent erected off the footpath, its flap open. A sign overhead boasted *Madame Zoee, Fortune-Teller and Mystic*.

A fortune-teller might well be a very tempting exhibition for anyone. Hurrying toward the tent, Richard poked his head inside, already preparing an apology for interrupting a customer's reading.

In the center of the cleared area, Evelyn sat at a red-covered table, sipping from a dented mug, while a robust woman in gypsy garb rubbed her back and spoke in low tones.

When a shadow fell across them, Evelyn turned to see her husband framed in the entryway. Her relief was instantaneous. "Richard," she choked out.

The cup of tea forgotten, she stood, her need to be held in his arms so she could feel completely safe overwhelming everything else. Whether they'd meant her harm or not, those men had frightened her.

"Evie." He reached her in two large strides, one arm encircling her waist to hold her close. Tenderly, he cupped her face with his other hand, peering down at her. "What happened?"

Unable to find her voice, the tears she'd managed to hold at bay would no longer be ignored and freely rolled down her cheeks. "I-I should have w-waited for Lucinda. I'm sorry."

He tucked her face against his chest. "Shh." His thumb made small circles to the base of her skull as he dropped a kiss to the top of her head.

As she raised her face to his, he met Madame Zoee's eyes. "I'm her husband."

The fortune-teller nodded briskly. "When I returned to my tent, two men were scaring your *jolie femme*." Scorn thickened her accented English. "Nasty *batards*, stinking of whiskey. My Harvey kicked them out, then followed to make sure they left."

Evelyn didn't miss the way Richard went still, tension locking his muscles. The soothing motion of his thumb paused for the barest of moments, before he resumed the gentle ministrations. "What men?"

Was he asking her or the fortune-teller? Either way, his stern expression didn't bode well for whoever those men were. "I don't know, although they did look somewhat familiar."

Richard's gaze returned to her, glinting with anger. "Did they hurt you?"

She shook her head. "I'm not sure that was their intent."

He led her back to the table and settled her into the chair, while Madame Zoee stepped outside. Taking her hands into his, he knelt at her feet. "Why do you think that?"

Evelyn searched her mind for the exact words they'd said to her. "They kept mentioning the fact I was yours, as if it was important to them."

Richard's expression darkened. "What did they say?"

"They recognized me as your wife, right away. Said you should take better care of me or I could get hurt. Or something like that. I'm sorry, I can't remember the exact words."

"They didn't touch you?"

She parted her lips in denial, then remembered the man's bruising grip. "The one with the scar grabbed me when I tripped."

His mouth flattened, something hard and cold brewing in the depths of his eyes. "One had a scar?"

"Yes. Across his cheek."

Richard abruptly stood, his nostrils flaring like a bull ready to charge. "I'm going to kill them."

"And I'm going to pretend I didn't hear that," a gruff voice called out from the tent entrance.

Evelyn peered around Richard's stiff frame and recognized Harrison Carter, strolling over to Madame Zoee's table.

He offered a tip of his Stetson. "Glad to see you're safe and sound, Missus Blackwood."

Richard gritted out between clenched teeth, "The Shaw brothers threatened her."

"Yeah, I talked with the fortune-teller and her husband. Quite an interesting couple. According to Madame Zoee, Harvey marched them off Galleria property. Mentioned one of the men had a nasty scar and a limp."

He sent Richard an arch look. "Didn't you shoot Grover Shaw in the leg last year?"

Richard produced a knowing smirk, though his eyes remained stormy. "Either the leg or the ass. Not sure which bullet was mine."

Evelyn blinked in wonder. She'd never seen the harder, lawman side of Richard before, a strength of duty he wore with ease. Understanding he was more than capable of protecting his townspeople, pride swelled within her heart.

How lucky I am.

As if reading her mind, Richard edged closer to her chair. His attention still on Harrison, he slipped a hand around the nape of her neck. The gentle stroke of his thumb against her skin soothed her frayed nerves.

Yet his voice harshened as he added, "Either Shaw gets near my wife again, next time that bullet goes right between his eyes. Right now, I'll settle for a horsewhipping and some answers."

Harrison scratched his stubbled jaw. "Want me to round up Frank or Joshua so we can pay them a little visit?"

"Ben and I went out to the smelter right after the fire." Richard paused in his caress, as if gathering his thoughts. "We had a little talk with the Shaws. Couldn't find anything other than noticing they'd mishandled the mules. Funny thing," he added, meeting Harrison's frown, "I didn't recognize any of the smelter workers. A surly bunch too."

"You think they hired desperadoes?"

He shrugged. "Wouldn't surprise me. Probably should check on that. We left Grover and Floyd with a warning but maybe another visit wouldn't be a bad idea."

Not liking this conversation at all, Evelyn clumsily gained her feet. "Now?" Still shaken from the scary encounter, she didn't want Richard to leave.

Their babe decided it was time to make its presence known and kicked her in the side. She gasped and palmed the spot.

Concern lined Richard's features. "What's wrong?"

The babe kicked again, but she was ready for it this time. Smiling, she took Richard's hand and laid it on her stomach, where their child stirred. "Someone's awake."

His eyes widened. "He's got quite a punch."

Evelyn huffed. "*She* thinks you should take me home instead of running off half-cocked. Those men will still be there tomorrow for your, er, horsewhip."

"Do as your lovely wife asked, Richard. We can talk at the jailhouse tomorrow after breakfast,"

Harrison advised. Not waiting for an answer, he exited the tent.

Home. It suddenly dawned on her how the tidy ranch she and Richard lived in did feel like home. The longing to curl up in front of a fire, within her husband's embrace, was exactly what she needed.

The babe undulated under his touch, the feeling such a miracle, that joyous laughter rose up within her and spilled over. Then her breath caught when familiar passion—a look she'd missed so much— flared in Richard's eyes.

An entirely different kind of need took hold of her.

His lips pursed enticingly. "Ready to go home?"

The intimacy in his softly spoken endearment wrapped around Evelyn like a caress. Excitement dried her voice to dust.

Nodding inanely, she let him help her to her feet and escort her from the tent.

Chapter 12

Richard brought the buggy to a stop as close to the ranch's front yard as he could get without horse hooves clomping over the rosebushes his aunt had so lovingly planted last month.

"Stay here. I'm going to stable the mare." Jumping down, he unhitched Cloud and led her to the barn, settling her with a scoop of oats before rushing back to Evelyn's side.

He swung her off the seat and into his arms, holding her suspended, her beautiful face inches from his, and indulged in a few kisses.

A feeling of rightness engulfed him.

She's meant to be mine.

Richard was more determined than ever to prove to Evelyn that she'd made the right decision in seeking him out.

To marry him.

The ranch was isolated, inasmuch as they had no immediate neighbors, though the main road from town came within yards of the fencing blocking off their land.

She allowed the intimacy, squirming a bit in his embrace. Thinking her modest reticence endearing, Richard released her lips and set her on her feet carefully, mindful of her condition, loving her warmth against him.

"Mmm," he purred in her ear.

Abruptly he swept her back into his arms and carried her up the path to the front door, managing the latch one-handed, unwilling to release her for even an instant.

Inside, he nuzzled her neck. "Alone at last."

Holding her tighter, he brought her into their bedroom. He'd tossed and turned beside her more than one night, wishing to behold her sprawled amongst the bedsheets waiting for him to make love to her, instead of curled next to him, fast asleep.

It was time to claim his wife, time to begin taking care of the woman who carried his child. Nothing was more important or more precious.

Shadows had begun to darken the corners of the room as Richard laid her on the bed. She stretched, unknowingly seductive, innocently appealing.

Not bothering to light the lantern sconce on the wall, he unbuttoned his shirt, studying her closely for any signs of unease, but finding only desire on her lovely face.

Her hand went to the front of her increasing gown. The soft green fabric was pretty, but her satiny skin surpassed everything else as she straightened, leaning back against the headboard.

Anticipation tightened his muscles as he waited for his first glimpse of Evelyn's luscious breasts, imagining them fuller now, with rosy nipples darker than their usual pale pink.

She slid the sleeves of her dress off her shoulders, then the straps of her chemise, baring her creamy flesh to his avid gaze, lush with impending motherhood.

"You're so beautiful." Dropping his shirt to the floor, he yanked at his trousers. Forgetting to unfasten them, he winced when the unyielding waistband caught on his hips. "Ouch."

Amusement danced in her eyes. "Please don't damage anything." Her voice lowered to a seductive timbre. "Husband."

As Evelyn claimed him with one softly spoken word, emotion roughened his reply. "I like the sound of that."

He toed off his boots and socks, leaving them where they lay atop his abandoned trousers and smalls. *Time to make this marriage a real one, in every way.*

Naked, he prowled toward her on hands and knees, awash in satisfaction when her eyes grew large, and her cheeks flushed anew.

She looked him over, visibly swallowing. "Oh, my. I had forgotten . . ."

"Forgotten what?" He stroked one of her shapely thighs then cupped the tender roundness where their child grew.

Evelyn's blush deepened. "How very manly you are," she whispered. "How strong, and—"

"Hungry." He kissed her bare shoulder. Raising his eyes to hers, he added, "Hungry for the woman I never forgot, never stopped wanting."

She clasped his neck with surprising strength, drawing him down until he hovered over her. "Show me," she demanded breathlessly. "Like you did the first time."

"What we gonna do? That's three, dammit." Floyd stomped around the confines of the cramped office, fury pouring off him.

Grover swiped a grimy sleeve over his perspiring face as he stared out into the furnace room where a few remaining men toiled. Beyond the open area, darkness should have brought some relief from the unrelenting summer heat, but the air felt dead and stifling.

Tomorrow a new load of ore should arrive from the Carter Mine, twice as much as they usually handled at once. Five more men would come with it, leading the mules and carts, staying on to work in the furnace and see it through the process.

Except word had reached Stoney, the floor boss, that several Carter miners refused to bring their minerals, and they'd be lucky to see one cartful. The bad news had hit Grover's ears minutes after he and Floyd had hitched their horses and gone inside.

Someone's been talkin'.

"We was countin' on that load," Floyd seethed. He punched at the wall behind the desk, leaving a divot, and drew back bloody knuckles. "Sumbitch!"

Cradling his injury, he stomped over to the corner barrel and plunged in his fist, ruining the only clean drinking water they had.

Ignoring Floyd's antics, Grover plotted silently. This late, nothing could be done. They'd have to wait until after they'd crushed and roasted what was left of the ore they'd received last week.

He'd personally doctored the ledgers, shorting the proceeds going back to the miners. Up until now, the system had worked, with no one the wiser and their coffers nicely growing.

If the promised minerals didn't arrive by cart soon, there wouldn't be enough bullion to send to Georgetown, resulting in low returns. Ultimately the Shaw Smelter could face bankruptcy.

It'd all started with that idiot Tipple's big mouth. The more he studied on it, the angrier Grover got.

"This blasted town," he began in a dangerous rumble. "Gossipin' fools, worse than a bunch of biddies. They got no business pullin' their ore. Where else're they gonna take it?"

He spun to face his brother—who still nursed his knuckles as if he were a snotty nosed runt instead of a grown man—and pushed him away from the water barrel, sending him into the same wall he'd punched. "*Think*, dammit. We need a plan."

Muttering, Floyd righted himself and dropped his uninjured hand to his holster. "Kill 'em all. Anyone git in our way, they's dead."

"Christ sakes, the law'd come after us and string us up if we start shootin'. Use that lump between your ears you call a brain."

Grover swung around to kick the office door shut, ignoring the curious looks from some of the workers in the furnace room. "Don't need nobody listenin', neither."

He stalked back to the desk, shuffling through the current ledger, searching for names. "We need to dole out some hard coaxin'." He jabbed at a few scribbled lines. "There. Washburn. One of 'em Stoney says pulled out. Sent his oldest boy over, too lily-livered to do it hisself."

"Ain't he only got one leg?" Floyd reached for a half-empty bottle of Jim Beam he'd been hoarding and pulled out the cork with his teeth.

He spat it on the cluttered floor. "Don't see why we can't bring a one-legged old man around to our way of thinkin'."

He took a long slug of the whiskey, then passed the bottle to Grover. "An' if he don't want to do business no more, who's to say he didn't fall, tryin' to get around, with him gimpy an' such?"

Floyd's grin turned predatory. "Hell, a man can break his neck out there at the mines."

Early next morning, Evelyn roused to the heat of Richard's unclothed body pressed along her back as she lay on her side. Her head rested in the crook of his arm. He'd draped the other across her waist.

The evidence of his growing arousal nudged her thigh as he scattered kisses over her neck and shoulders.

She laughed softly. "You're insatiable."

"Only with you," he murmured into her ear.

The memory of their first real intimacies together as husband and wife caused a now-familiar ache deep inside her. Delicious shivers assailed her when she recalled how he'd given her pleasure with his hands and mouth, *twice*, before joining their bodies in passion.

After the third time he'd made love to her, she'd collapsed against him, the steady beat of his heart under her ear lulling her to sleep. Although they'd been married for a few months now, last night was the first time Evelyn had actually felt like a true wife.

Palming her breast, Richard caressed her ardently, his other hand trailing down her body until he reached her thighs. She moaned at the feel of his fingers feathering across her sensitive bud, arching when they slipped inside.

His throaty chuckle sent goosebumps over her skin. "So wet. Do you want me, sweet Evie?"

"Yes." The word tore from her throat as she trembled in anticipation. How could she want him so badly after having him several times during the night?

Richard's sensual touch grew urgent, increasing her desire. Combined with his soft words of praise and encouragement, she hovered on the edge of another release.

In the next breath he shifted, now holding her leg at a careful angle. When he slid into her body, a needy groan sounded from behind her.

Recalling how energetic their couplings used to be back in Baltimore, Evelyn adored this newfound tenderness in their lovemaking even more, because of the babe nestled protectively in her womb.

With long, unhurried strokes, cradling her gently, he nuzzled her neck, bringing them both to a blissful completion.

She lay quietly in his embrace for many minutes as their labored breathing calmed.

Finally, Richard eased away. "Morning, Wife."

Yawning, she turned to face him as he lay on his back. "Morning, Husband."

Staring into her eyes, he thumbed a spot on her cheek where his short whiskers had rubbed her skin. "Sorry, I'm bristly."

"Don't care." She fingered the roughness on his face, enjoying those morning prickles. "It's a fine way to waken, in my opinion."

"Your opinion is the only one that matters." He drew back to study her in the soft light coming in through the muslin curtains. "How do you feel?"

"As if I fell into heaven, head-first." Her frank admission startled her, but it was true.

Never had she known such joy in her life. Nor could she have ever imagined—when she first boarded the train in Baltimore, miserable in heart and sore in body—that she'd find such contentment in motherhood and marriage.

The growing bond between her and Richard was more than Evelyn ever dreamed it could be. Up until this moment, the coldness in her parents' union had been her only guide.

Snuggled up to her husband in the warm bed, golden beams of sunlight touching their room, Evelyn could admit what she felt might be love. Whether or not Richard felt it too was something to ponder silently. Doubtful he was ready for more than duty and responsibility. Though he cared for her, wanted her, neither guaranteed what she'd always considered true love to be.

Granny Nia had told her love would come. Evelyn believed that promise with her whole heart.

Her reverie was disrupted by Richard drawing her in for a few more kisses, before he sat up and swung his legs over the side of the bed. "I'm headed to the jailhouse. Might have to ride out to the smelter later this morning and have another little chat with the Shaws."

"I don't want you to do that." Evelyn tugged the blanket to her breasts, covering her nakedness. Thinking of him facing those two horrid men again sent cold panic over every inch of her body. "It's a bad idea."

He looked vaguely insulted as he stood and retrieved his clothes. "You think I'm not capable of dealing with a couple of lowlife hucksters?"

"They're unpredictable, Richard. Unstable and downright mean. You can't reason with men like that."

"I *am* a lawman. I can handle myself."

She anxiously chewed on her lip until it stung. Physical violence was foreign to her and to the way she'd been brought up in her father's house. Stern, inflexible coldness was Horace Calhoun's way, his cruel words and disapproving expression all he'd needed to control her and Mother.

"Promise you won't do anything rash."

"Promise." He eyed her thoughtfully. "Do you want me to ask Vivian or Aunt Lucinda to come sit with you?"

"Lord, no." She suspected both women had better things to do than perform nursemaid duties. "I'm a grown woman," she reprimanded.

One side of his mouth curled teasingly as he looked her over. "I'm very aware of that. *My woman*." His smile faded into sober intent. "As such, your safety is my top priority."

The possessiveness in her husband's tone made her tingle with pleasure. Never had Evelyn dreamed she'd end up as a wife to such a brave, honorable man. "I'll be perfectly fine by myself, Richard."

Fully dressed, he approached their bed and leaned in for a quick kiss. "Stay alert. If you see anyone suspicious near the cabin, get your pretty self inside and lock the door. And don't be afraid to use the rifle if you need to."

Chapter 13

Her thoughts filled with her husband and the amazing night they'd shared, Evelyn kept her worry at bay by tidying up the ranch house. Richard's aunt had shown her a narrow cupboard in the kitchen where tins of carnauba wax and linseed oil were kept.

Recalling Lucinda's instruction on how to mix the wax and oil to produce the best polishing results, Evelyn dabbed both sparingly on a soft linen and rubbed the strongly scented emollients together. With some sweat and effort, she soon had every surface shining, not a speck of dust left behind.

Yet her brain refused to release images of Richard and the Shaw brothers, coming to blows. *I need more to do.*

"Maybe I'll cook something," she mused, peering into the pantry for ideas. Spotting a sack of dried beans, she was reminded of how the family chef in Baltimore prepared poached fowl in bean gravy. Maybe she couldn't make the gravy but surely roasting or boiling a chicken couldn't be all that complicated.

Richard loved chicken, this she already knew. How hard could it be to roast a bird? All she had to do was catch one, wring its neck, and pluck it. Ticking off the process on her fingers, Evelyn brightened. Two of the brown chickens in the coop out back had stopped laying.

Perfect for cooking.

Bernadette, the housekeeper Father employed in Baltimore, would dunk a chicken in scalding water to loosen the feathers, making them easier to pluck out.

I can do this.

An hour later, perspiring heavily and exhausted from chasing one very angry, squawking hen, Evelyn sank to the rough grass several yards from the coop entrance and wiped her face with the hem of her gown. Her heart pounded too fast to be good for the babe and sweat plastered her hair to her neck. The chicken strutted around in circles, clucking triumphantly at having thwarted death.

"Stupid bird." She scowled at the irritating thing.

If she couldn't even get her hands on the feathered beast, how on earth was she to prepare Richard's favorite dinner?

Groaning, Evelyn got to her feet, brushing off her skirts, determined to try again. As she advanced, the hen hopped from foot to foot, its beady eyes watching her suspiciously.

Three yards away, then two . . .

With a series of loud squawks, the bird flapped its wings and flew up into the branches of a nearby tree. There it perched, its narrow head bobbing as if in defiance.

"No!" She stomped her foot hard, forgetting she wore only flimsy house slippers. Her heel came down on a pointed stone. Instant pain had her hopping around in a ridiculously similar pantomime of the dratted chicken.

She swore it cackled in amusement.

A low, raspy salutation brought her up short. "What you doing, *bebe*?"

Evelyn shrieked, spun unsteadily, and gaped at the sight of Madame Zoee, leaning on the porch railing as if she had not a care in the world.

In her colorful scarves and beads, she looked exotic and as out-of-place as a peacock in a cow pasture.

"M-Madame," Evelyn stuttered.

The fortune-teller straightened and swayed gracefully toward her. She laid the back of a beringed hand across Evelyn's forehead, eyeing her critically. "Still pale, eh?" She jerked her chin toward the thick branch where Richard's would-be dinner squatted.

"That how you learned to catch a *poule*, up in a tree?" Her tongue clicked reprovingly against pearly white teeth. "Come, I show you how to get this bird."

Evelyn's brows scrunched in curiosity. "What are you doing here?"

"I found your pretty gloves on the floor of my tent and wanted to return them to you. How fortunate to see your man *le depute* Blackwood as I came into town. He provided me with directions."

Zoee fanned herself vigorously, causing Evelyn to giggle. "Such a manly form!" She held out the lacy gloves Evelyn had worn the opening day of the Menagerie.

"Thank you, Madame." She paused. "Would you like a cup of coffee?"

"*Oui*, that would be lovely. But first, we catch your bird. And I show you how to deal with *un petit batard.*"

Evelyn nodded eagerly. "I would very much appreciate the help, Madame."

"For you, I am *Mere* Zoee." She leaned in to press a warm kiss to Evelyn's temple. "We catch the bird and pluck all the feathers. You plan to cook it today, yes?"

"Oh, yes." She glared at the hen as it preened its wings. "I want to cook that *petit batard* like you would not believe. Except I don't know how."

Zoee threw back her head and shouted with laughter. Wiping at her eyes, she made for the coop where the chicken feed was kept. "Good thing I stopped by."

Richard stomped up the steps of Little Creede's jail. The wrath he'd managed to keep under control all night—for Evelyn's benefit—heated to a flat-out boil. The Shaws had laid their hands on his wife. Uncaring of her delicate condition, they'd frightened her.

And for that, they're gonna pay.

Edward Coogan was nailing a wanted poster on the wall as Richard entered the jailhouse office. The young man's grandfather was Rocky Gulch's sheriff, and since he'd vouched for his grandson's character, Joshua hired him despite his young age. The kid seemed competent enough.

The elder Coogan planned to retire as soon as Richard was able to take over for him. *If not for Grandpa August's death, I'd already be resettled there.*

He felt bad about making them wait, but he still had some time before he reported to his new post and position. Once the saloon Sam Singleton and Knight Gleason were constructing in Rocky Gulch was completed, the town's population would grow fast.

While fulfilling his duties as Gleason's former head of security, Sam had married the Galleria's prior kitchen worker, Izzy McDougall, and the happy couple now lived in Rocky Gulch with their young daughter.

Located in a prime spot along Main Street, the saloon's grand opening was expected early next spring, and Richard planned to be positioned there by then.

Edward turned to him. "Morning, sir."

'Mornin'," Richard muttered.

He strode to his desk and tugged open the middle drawer where he collected various items of note. No matter how many times he told the kid to call him by his first name, Coogan continued to address him more formally, along with the rest of his elders. His impeccable manners were downright annoying.

"Something wrong?" Edward asked. "You seem riled this morning."

"Had some trouble with the Shaws last evening." A knifelike pain shot through his temples, and he unclenched his teeth, moving his lower jaw from side to side to ease the tension.

"What kind of trouble?"

Finding the information he was looking for, Richard fisted the piece of paper in his hand and met the young deputy's questioning gaze. "They approached my wife and scared her. I suspect the threat was meant for me."

Edward's eyes widened. He gave a low whistle. "That was a stupid thing to do."

"Yep."

"Weren't they involved in the kidnapping of Mister Singleton's wife a while back?"

"They were, but we had nothing to hold them on since the man who actually took her was killed during the rescue. The Shaws claimed they didn't realize she was being held against her will, and we couldn't prove otherwise."

"Didn't you shoot one of 'em?"

Richard chuckled. "Well, bullets were surely flying."

"Wish I could have been there."

"Next time, kid." He headed for the front door. "I'm gonna telegraph an associate in Chicago to do some digging on these two. We found out they ran with criminal elements before moving out West. I need to know everything about them. Then I'm riding out to the smelter to make it clear they're never to get near my wife again."

"They're not at the smelter, sir."

Richard paused. "What?"

"I saw them at the mercantile, not more than twenty minutes ago."

"Even better." Richard yanked the door open. Recalling Evelyn's fear inside the fortune-teller's tent, a hard knot of fury tightened his muscles. "I'll deal with these fools first."

"I could send the telegram for you, if you like," Edward offered.

"Thanks." He handed over the contact information. "Abner Dale runs the place. Let him know it's for me. He'll get the job done."

Not waiting for an answer, Richard strode outside. The street bustled with activity as he purposely crossed to the mercantile.

Catherine Carter, owner of The Miner Stage House, drew near, supervising a boy who pulled a cart filled with what appeared to be foodstuffs for her restaurant.

Dressed in deep green from head to toe, she cut a stylish picture as always. "Morning, Richard."

For courtesy's sake, he tipped his hat. "Morning, Catherine." He could hear the anger in his tone. *Dammit.*

She paused, one hand on the boy's shoulder, and raised an eyebrow. "Trouble?"

He blew out a frustrated breath, unwilling to upset her. Catherine was not like other women. Having led a rougher life than most, she had a way of sizing up a situation with an ease others lacked. That sort of talent made her a great businesswoman, running one of the most popular hotels and eateries within a hundred miles. It also made her the perfect wife for Frank Carter, Lucinda's oldest son, which meant the Carter siblings were Richard's cousins of sorts.

Slowing, he forced what he hoped was a more friendly smile. "Nothing to worry about." Not wanting the Shaws to sneak out of town while he was distracted, he kept their horses in his peripheral vision. "Have a good day, Catherine."

He eyed the boy, recognizing one of the bank teller's young'uns. "You listen good to Missus Carter, y'hear?"

"Yes'm, sir," the lad mumbled, his freckled cheeks blooming red.

Feeling their eyes on his back, Richard hurried down the street. Several curious townsfolk called out greetings which he returned without diverting his attention from the target, too intent on his objective to worry about gossip.

Though Little Creede was a fast-growing boomtown, sometimes it still felt too small, with everybody in everyone else's business.

Richard spotted the Shaws through the large display window of the mercantile. The owners, Silas and Betsey Loman, had installed the valuable glass last summer. At the time they'd celebrated their new purchase by offering free pastries and lemonade to Little Creede's townsfolk.

Betsey kept the window spotless, wiping it down every morning before the store opened. If anything happened to that piece of glass as a result of Richard's dealings with the two dregs of society inside, he'd never forgive himself. Not to mention weeks ago, she'd reported her suspicion about Floyd Shaw stealing smaller items every time he came inside.

I've got to get them to come out.

He entered quietly, noting how Betsy watched worriedly as both Shaws swaggered up and down the narrow aisle.

Grover came to an abrupt stop when he spotted Richard. Anger darkened the man's expression.

Probably still sore over taking a bullet to his ass. Judging by his unsteady gait, the man had a permanent limp from his leg wound too. Served the fool right. "Mornin', Betsey."

"Good morning, Richard. Can I help you with anything?"

He shook his head, crossing the room toward Grover. "No, ma'am. Just here taking care of some personal business."

Floyd noticed him and hurriedly joined his brother, his nasty glower rendering him even uglier as his right hand hovered over the gun at his hip.

Richard stopped a few feet from the two. Whipping his Colt from his holster, he took aim at the Shaws. "I wouldn't do that, Floyd," he drawled. "You'll be dead before your fingers touch steel."

Grover's bushy brows drew down, the tips nearly touching his nose. "What d'ya want, Blackwood?"

"Hands in the air, boys," he demanded through gritted teeth. A tense minute of silence filled the room until Grover raised his arms, followed by his brother doing the same. "Now, step outside."

"What for?" Floyd shifted nervously.

Richard motioned his gun's barrel toward the door. "Move. Now!"

A mean smirk distorted Grover's scarred face as he casually strolled to the exit. "Is this about your pretty little wife?"

Fury twisted Richard's gut, but he ignored it, all his concentration on the danger in front of him. "Shut up and keep walking."

Once they'd cleared the mercantile doors, Richard herded them further down the street where they would do less damage. "That's far enough."

Grover and Floyd turned back to him with matching calculating expressions. "We didn't touch the lady," Floyd groused.

"Shut up, Floyd," Grover snapped, never taking his eyes off Richard. "You got nothin' on us, Blackwood. We never laid a hand on your lovely woman."

The way the man's tone caressed the word *lovely* set Richard even further on edge. "Toss your guns to the ground."

"What for?" Floyd complained. "We ain't done nothin'."

Richard arched a brow. "Your brother always whine like a little girl?"

"Do as the man says, Floyd." Grover tossed his gun down. Still grumbling, his brother did the same.

"Now kick them away." Richard maintained a steady bead on the two.

Visibly unhappy, they complied with his request. "You're attractin' a crowd, deputy." Grover smirked. "Don't think you can shoot us in cold blood."

Richard hadn't missed how half the town stopped what they were doing to watch the action in the street. Nothing could be done about that. The Shaws were about to experience the dangers of harassing his wife and anyone else in his family. "Didn't plan on it."

Keeping a keen eye on them, he unfastened his gun belt and leg ties, then knelt and laid everything on the ground. "I'm not here as Little Creede's deputy."

Standing to his full height, he unpinned the badge on his chest and tossed it next to his holster. "I'm here as a husband who's going to beat the ever-living tar out of you for scaring my wife."

He circled the two, waiting for the first one to attack. "C'mon now." He waved them over. "Show me what you got."

Floyd snorted derisively. "You think you can take us both on?"

"Reckon so."

Richard braced himself for battle. The hush that fell over the town was deafening, not even a bird singing as if attuned to incipient violence.

Floyd made the first move, but Richard was ready for him and took him out with one hard punch to the jaw. The man dropped faster than a load of lead and didn't get back up.

Out. Cold.

Richard chuckled, meeting Grover's glare. "Looks like it's just you and me, asshole."

Grover lunged for him and he ducked, barely missing the meaty fist headed for his face. Using the momentum of his body, Richard popped back up, tossing the big man over his shoulder where he hit the ground with a loud thud. If it hadn't been for the slight limp where Grover had been shot, the blow might have landed.

Spinning on a bootheel, Richard faced his opponent as he climbed back to his feet.

Rage mottled Grover's face. He crouched and charged, head-butting Richard in the midsection, both of them landing in a heap of flying fists.

Scrambling to his knees, Grover knuckled Richard's shirt and swung his other fist toward his throat.

Richard jerked to the side, catching only a glancing tap to the chin as he propelled his body to the left.

Rolling Grover beneath him, Richard drew back, hitting his intended target with a hard punch to the nose.

Grover let out an angry howl and twisted his body away, until he was able to fling Richard off.

Richard jumped to his feet, satisfied at the blood dripping from Grover's nostrils. His upper lip curled in contempt. "That all you got?"

"You bastard," Grover snarled, clumsily swaying as he stood. He swiped at the blood with his shirt sleeve. "I'm gonna kill you."

"You can try." Richard let fly again, this time connecting with Grover's jaw, making him stagger.

Recovering fast, he took another swing at Richard, smacking him in the eye. "Gonna mark you up good, Blackwood," he wheezed.

That'll leave a bruise. Shaking off the pain, Richard countered with a solid uppercut to his opponent's scarred cheek.

Bellowing furiously, Grover tackled him again, tumbling them to the ground where they rolled and pummeled each other until they were both heaving for breath.

Townsfolk had started calling out encouragement to Richard, the women scandalized, the men hollering and jostling each other.

"I got money on ya, Blackwood!" someone boomed from somewhere behind him.

"Me too," another called. "Flatten that idjit!"

Cracking a stiff grin, Richard gained his feet and waited for Grover to steady himself, before plowing his fist into a gut that'd seen too many beers.

Grover's fury must have outweighed the damage his body sustained because he retaliated with a vicious swing.

When Richard flung an arm up to block the blow, Grover slammed his other fist into his stomach instead. The hit robbed his breath for a moment. "Smooth move," he panted, ducking another blow.

Grover wasn't the dumber Shaw. But Richard was smarter and more skilled. It was time to put the brothers in their place. Already, he could hear Floyd moaning as he roused.

Straightening, Richard dealt two more hits to Grover's midsection.

As Shaw doubled over, huffing with exertion, Richard clenched both fists into a single weapon and brought it down on the back of his head.

Sprawled face first onto the dusty street, Grover didn't get back up.

A mixture of voices suddenly called out warnings. "Behind you, Deputy!"

"Watch out!"

"He's got his gun!"

At the same time a familiar voice grated out, "Drop it."

Richard spun around and found Dub had shoved his pistol into Floyd's temple, forcing him to uncock and release his own gun. It fell harmlessly to the ground.

His uncle shrugged, a glint of humor in his eyes. "Catherine said you might need an extra hand."

Richard snorted. "Appreciate it."

Grover groaned and rolled, belly up, struggling to rise. Richard grabbed the front of his shirt and hauled him to his feet.

He shoved Grover toward his brother, who caught him weakly, both stumbling in the dusty street. Already, bruises had formed on their faces.

Ignoring his own sore muscles and aching eye, Richard advanced threateningly. "If I ever see you two anywhere near my wife, I'm gonna forget I'm a lawman."

He paused for effect, looming over both, using his superior height to intimidate. "You understand me?"

"Yeah, yeah. We understand," Floyd said sullenly.

"Good. Now get the hell out of my town."

Chapter 14

Evelyn laid down her fork and leaned back in her chair with a satisfied sigh. "You are a wonderful cook, *Mere* Zoee."

"*Moi*? I did nothing but guide you, *bebe*. You are learning fast." The fortune-teller licked at her thumb delicately, the rings she wore glittering in the bright kitchen.

Never having seen anyone boasting jewelry on every finger, Evelyn was fascinated. "Your rings are lovely. Have they meaning in your work?"

Zoee wiped her hands on a napkin. "In a way. Always I have worn them. Some belonged to my beloved *maman*. One, my *grandpere* wore."

She wriggled a middle finger, on which resided an intricately etched silver band. "He was a skinny man of much wisdom. He could look into your eyes and know your life path. He passed on much of this. *Maman* did not approve, but I embraced all he shared."

She reached for Evelyn's hand and turned it palm-up, studying it, while Evelyn held her breath and wondered what on earth a mere hand could reveal.

"Soft and *tres elegante*," Zoee commented, tracing the middle of Evelyn's palm with her thumb. "Ah, a fresh callus! More than one." She looked up from her perusal. "You have a determined heart. I did not have to see you dash through the dust after that stupid yet quite tasty *poule*, to know this."

"He was tasty, for sure," Evelyn said, amused, yet her mirth faded at the older woman's intense examination of her palm. "What do you see, *Mere*?" she whispered.

Zoee traced another path. "A palm has many lines and meanings hidden from most eyes. These lines speak of life, of heart. Ridges show strengths and weaknesses."

"I remember hearing a palm reader could figure out when someone would die."

"It doesn't work that way." Zoee met Evelyn's worried expression frankly. "I can divine your past, provide advice for your future. Maybe good or not. But one does not predict *la morte*, you understand?" She gave a shudder. "And who would want to?"

"Would you, can you tell me some things?" Lord, she didn't even know how to ask.

Perhaps this was nothing more than a sitting room game, a pastime to take her mind off whatever trouble Richard might be getting himself into. But looking into the nearly black gaze of this woman who was far more experienced in life, who'd already proved herself so kind and caring, Evelyn knew she could trust her.

"*Oui, ma petite*. There are things I can share."

Removing his hat to knock the dust off, Richard grimaced at the sight of his swollen knuckles. Pausing at the barn door, he pulled his bandana from his back pocket, not very fresh but all he had. He strode to the horse trough and dunked the wrinkled fabric, using the wettest end to wipe off what damage he could.

He'd examined himself in Betsey's sparkling glass window, relieved his eye didn't look too bad. Maybe Evelyn wouldn't notice.

He scoffed at the thought. *She'll notice all right, then worry.*

He filled a feed pail with more water to soak the bandana, mopping off what grime and sweat he could reach.

Retrieving Cloud from where he'd ground-hitched her, he crooned to the high-spirited paint mare as he led her to her stall, ladling oats into her bin. With his lady munching happily, Richard headed to the house, a fast peek into the front window revealing Evelyn curled up on the sofa with her embroidery hoop.

He didn't want to explain what'd happened in town. He also knew deliberately keeping it from her was a mistake.

If she asks, I'll tell her.

Leaving his dirty boots and socks on the porch, he headed into the sitting room. "I'm home." As she rose a bit unsteadily, he hastened to her side. "Don't get up, Evie."

"You'll want dinner," she insisted, sinking down onto the sofa cushions. Then with a gasp she grabbed his sleeve. "Richard, your hands!" Her gaze narrowed on his face. "And your eye, what did you do?"

"It was nothing." At her suspicious regard, he sighed heavily. "I might have had an altercation," he hedged. Like as not, he'd give in to telling her everything since she'd already known of his plans to pay the Shaws a visit.

"You fought those beastly brothers, didn't you?" Evelyn accused.

"I was provoked." He hesitated, wondering if he should mention he'd more or less started it all by laying down his guns and encouraging the idiots to come at him first.

"Oh, Richard." She leaned back on her seat, staring at his bruises. "They're going to crack open if you tighten your fist. And just how were you provoked?"

Resigned, he explained how he'd confronted the brothers after he'd spotted them stomping through the mercantile, worrying Betsey Loman.

"I ended up beating both their worthless hides. I would have liked to drag them to jail, but as a lawman I'm supposed to uphold the Sixth Amendment which pretty much states someone is presumed innocent until fairly tried in a court of law."

He shrugged nonchalantly. "I took off my badge and guns before I pounded on them."

"Well, that's something at least. Is Betsey all right?"

"She's fine." Knowing his wife had a soft spot for Betsey—hell, most of the town—made him want to burst with pride.

"So," he began, eager to take her mind off his bruises, "What's in the pot?"

"I made chicken fricassee."

Richard blinked at her proud statement. "You did? Where'd you get a chicken?"

Surely, she didn't actually begin with a live bird.

"I managed, with help. I had a visit from Madame Zoee. From the Menagerie," she clarified. "She came by to return my gloves. I'd been chasing that stupid chicken all around the yard, so she helped me get it ready to, um, cook, and stayed to show me how to fricassee."

Her expression grew unsure. "Was it all right to take one of the chickens?"

Richard reached for her. "Of course." He cuddled her close. "I saw Madame in town. I'm glad she stopped in to visit. Nice of her to help too."

"I saved three pieces for you." Evelyn tugged at his hand, eliciting a covert wince when her grip caught his knuckles. "And there's pandowdy for dessert."

Richard allowed himself to be hustled into the kitchen. "What kind?"

"Well, I didn't have enough peaches and only two apples, so I used both."

He guided her to a chair. "Sit down, Evie. I can serve myself."

While she rested at the table, he collected the pot from the stove and placed it in the middle of the table.

Sniffing appreciatively, he lifted the lid, uncovering golden-browned chicken. Not bothering with a fork, he dug in, helping himself to a leg.

"Delicious," he mumbled around mouthfuls of the tender, buttery meat.

Spying the dessert platter, he greedily eyed the pandowdy. "Did Madame Fortune-Teller also help you with dessert?"

No, indeed." Evelyn fluffed her hair, looking superior. "I remembered my lessons with Mary Rush and made it by myself."

"That's my girl."

For a few minutes silence reigned in the warm kitchen as he finished the chicken and started on a serving of pandowdy, humming in approval at the taste of sugared fruit. When he went for a third slice, Evelyn snatched the platter out of his reach. "No, you don't. I'm saving the rest for Vivian."

"Vivian Lang?"

"Yes. She's coming by tomorrow. Bringing little Isiah too. Well, I hope she does. Though she also mentioned the loan of some nursery furnishings, so her hands might be full."

Evelyn replaced the cover on the dessert platter. "I think it helps me prepare for the babe if I'm around children. And I'm to visit Maggie at the Galleria when she and Robert come to town with young Duncan."

Richard frowned, not liking the idea of Evelyn in Little Creede when the Shaws were still around, likely seeking some sort of retribution. He leaned across the table to snare one of his wife's hands. "Promise me you'll not try to travel to town by yourself."

He shot a pointed glance toward her expanding waistline. With only a few more months to go before the birth of their child, she ought to be confining herself to the ranch house, especially in this endless summer heat.

Her fingers tightened on his as her expression lost its brightness. "I'm quite well. Unless you're concerned about something else?"

"Shaws," he all but growled.

"Surely you don't think those men will come back. Why on earth would they return after you ran them out? Although," she mused aloud, then her lips thinned, her expression shadowing.

"Although, what?"

"It's nothing," she demurred, looking away. "Just something Madame Zoee said."

He lifted her chin until her eyes met his. "Tell me."

Evelyn huffed. "Oh, you know these fortune-tellers. They like to be theatrical and such. She just said I needed to be careful because she doesn't trust the Shaws. Told me they have evil in their hearts."

Don't need to be a fortune-teller to know that. "I agree."

"She also said I should keep my man close."

"Again, I agree." He was determined to protect her and the babe from any threats. "You tell me if anything, however small, becomes a worry."

She nodded. "Of course."

The next morning, Evelyn prepared a fresh pot of coffee and set out what remained of the pandowdy, eyeing the platter with amused resignation. Richard had certainly eaten his fill, but there was plenty left over.

It had been Vivian's habit to stop by now and then, usually with sweet toddler Isiah, to visit the morning away. Evelyn appreciated the womanly company greatly. Spending time with Isiah offered much-needed exposure to youngsters and their childish whims.

This visit, Vivian had offered to bring some of Isiah's swaddling clothes. Retta Carter had already donated a stack of everything from sleeping gowns to diapers, even several sets of darling, tiny slippers and shoes. Catherine Carter had sent over more increasing dresses and necessaries from her confinement with three-year-old Charity.

Evelyn found her new family's continuing kindness overwhelming at times but was so grateful for each who had taken the time to instruct, help out, visit, and often simply listen to her worries.

She smoothed the skirt of her gown, one she had brought from back East, absently noting its tightness around her midsection. Perhaps, instead of risking Catherine's fashionable outfits in the pursuit of housework, the fabric could be let out in order for her to get a few more months' use, a pragmatism that put a grin on her face at the thought of taking up needle and thread for something other than embroidering posies on a pillow. If she ruined the seams, then so be it.

How I have changed.

Cooking and baking, an ongoing adventure, was something she was growing to enjoy. Cleaning had remained a chore, though she was getting better.

Her darling husband had only teased her once, when she accidentally buffed the kitchen table with butter, thinking it would have the wood shining bright. Instead, it had attracted all manner of revolting bugs.

It'll be a while before I live that down, she thought with humor, recalling how her mistake had prompted Lucinda to reveal the wonders of combining beeswax and linseed oil.

Perhaps her finest achievement lay in the garden, for over the last month her skills had improved greatly. No longer did she rip up poor, unsuspecting vegetables. Now she enjoyed what time she spent with the crops.

The satisfaction of a task, done by her own efforts, had become vital to her as a wife. The future stretched out before her, fulfilling and warmly content, all because she'd found her own self-confidence.

A knock at the front door had her rising to her feet too fast, and she grabbed at the back of her chair. Drawing in a steadying breath, Evelyn plodded to the door, readying a smile for Vivian.

Two children stood on the porch instead of Sheriff Lang's friendly wife and adorable tot. At the end of the front yard sat a buggy, the horse unbridled, grazing contentedly.

The boy, who wore faded trousers and a neatly pressed shirt, stepped forward. Black hair flopped over a wide, smooth forehead, framing high cheekbones and deep blue eyes. "Morning, Missus Blackwood. Remember me? I'm Nate Lang."

He nodded toward his younger companion, a familiar-looking, slender girl in a pinafore, wearing dust on her upturned nose and tangles in her pale-yellow hair, braided hastily into one long plait. "This is my cousin Addie. She's visiting us for the week."

"Yes, of course, Retta's daughter. Nice to see you both."

Nate held out a valise. "My ma sent over some things. A few more dresses she says you'll soon need. She also said to mention Uncle Harrison's got a cradle for you and he'll bring it over later on today."

He couldn't have been more than eleven or twelve, but those blue eyes held a maturity beyond his years.

Addie's grin revealed a missing front tooth, while her unabashed curiosity latched on to Evelyn's distended abdomen with feminine delight.

"When's your babe comin'? What're you gonna name her? We need more girls around these parts. Aunt Vivian says Isiah doesn't know how to use the potty and he cries a lot." She stretched out a grimy hand. "Can I feel if it's kickin'? Mama says babes hurt comin' out. Do they hurt goin' in?"

Nate groaned. "Addie, hush yourself." He pushed her behind him and restrained her there. "Sorry, ma'am. My cousin doesn't know about silence being golden and all."

While the little girl tried to squirm away, he mumbled, "Ma had to take my brother to see the doc this morning. He's got an earache and he won't use—" He shuffled his feet, red-faced. "Well, she had to put a diaper back on him."

"I understand," Evelyn managed, torn between dignity and the urge to belly laugh at Addie's rambling compounded by Nate's attempts to shut her up.

"Please come on inside." She swung the door wider, impressed by the way Nate politely held it open for her and Addie to enter first.

Ushering them both into the sitting room, Evelyn sank down into the armchair while Addie skipped around the room, peeking into corners. "Everything's so pretty in here. Grandpa Dub never put flowers on the tables or hung lace in the windows. Grandma says he was a heathen until she tamed him."

Nate poked her in the ribs. "If anyone's a heathen around these parts, it's you."

"Am not." Addie poked him back. "Mama says I'll be a lady soon."

"Maybe when Bonney Creek dries up," he taunted.

As Addie opened her mouth to screech, Evelyn hastily rose and got between them. "You know, there's milk and pandowdy in the kitchen."

Instantly the bickering cousins broke apart. "Peach?" Nate asked hopefully.

"Apple's better," Addie informed him in a haughty voice, though she jumped up and down.

"Well, you're in luck, because I made it with apples and peaches." Evelyn pointed toward the table and the plates she had set out in anticipation of Vivian's visit. "I'll get the milk."

A few minutes later, with both children digging into their treat in between gulps of milk, Evelyn opened the valise. In addition to the promised swaddling garments, she unearthed three dresses and a nightshift.

"Oh, these are lovely," she exclaimed, shaking them out over her lap. "What wonderful colors."

"They were Aunt Catherine's, first," Addie informed her through a mouthful of pastry. She swallowed the huge bite, adding, "Auntie is a fashion pate."

It took all of Evelyn's composure not to react to the child's declaration. "You mean *plate*, correct? Because a pate is a bald head," she intoned somberly, setting both children into giggling fits.

"Auntie's not *bald*! She has fire in her hair. I heard Uncle Frank say it, right before he bent her over his knee and kissed her." Addie tugged on her tangled braid. "I wish I had fire in *my* hair."

Evelyn set aside the nightshift she'd been admiring, folding the soft white batiste carefully. "Your hair is pure sunlight, Miss Addie. One day you'll be quite thankful for the color."

As the blushing girl fidgeted in her chair, Evelyn took note of the affectionate way her cousin watched her, giving Addie's shoulder a squeeze that had her beaming again. These children were sweet to each other, with Nate adopting a teasing yet protective bent toward Addie.

I hope my babe is so readily accepted.

"Well now," Evelyn said, eyeing the platter, "we have one piece left. I can either split it in half or you can take pity on your mother and deliver the last serving to her."

"Let's eat it." Addie pushed at Nate when he clapped a hand over her mouth to shush her.

"We can bring it to Ma. Peach is her favorite," he said, ignoring his cousin's attempts to wriggle free. Addie paused, her expression going sly.

Suddenly Nate let her go and wiped his palm on the seat of his trousers. At Evelyn's raised eyebrow, he gave his cousin a disgruntled glare. "She licked me."

"Oh, goodness." She tried and failed to hold in laughter, collapsing back onto her chair. "You two are quite the entertainers."

Addie snorted, her elbow jostling Nate off-balance. "He had it coming."

Scooping the pandowdy into a bowl, Evelyn covered it with a towel. "Can I depend on you to deliver this safely without eating any of it?" She directed the question to both, though her attention remained on Addie.

Those thin shoulders stiffened. "Yes'm." Then she brightened. "If you make it again can Nate and me have some?"

"Nate and I," Evelyn corrected her gently.

Addie blinked. "What about y'all?"

Shaking his head, Nate exhaled noisily. "C'mon, heathen." He pushed his cousin toward the tiny foyer as Evelyn followed with the bowl.

She held it out, and he took it. "I'll bring it to Ma, Missus Blackwood. Thank you kindly."

An abrupt knock on the front door startled them. Evelyn frowned. "Maybe your mother decided to stop by after all."

"No, ma'am, not without the buggy."

Another hard knock rattled the door. Uneasy, she motioned the children back into the sitting room. "Stay there."

They both nodded, Addie huddling closer to Nate's side.

A narrow window to the left of the door only provided a view of a man's arm and part of a battered hat. She recognized neither.

I don't like this.

At the sound of a pounding fist, she jumped. Glancing behind to assure the children were out of sight, Evelyn reached for the rifle Richard kept nearby. She'd never shot a gun in her life, but perhaps the sight of her pointing one would be enough to deter a trespasser.

Clutching the weapon, prepared to scare off any unwelcome visitors, she unhooked the latch and swung the door open. Her jaw dropped as she took in the sight planted on her porch.

Good gracious. She propped the rifle against the wall next to her before shock caused her to drop it.

Seen up close, the man was vaguely familiar, tall and broad shouldered, long-legged, with a slightly crooked nose. A thatch of brown hair threaded with gray poked out beneath the stained hat he wore.

But it was the woman trembling next to him that caught and held Evelyn's attention and rapidly growing dismay. Her clothes were badly wrinkled, one long sleeve coming loose at the shoulder. Her hair hung in her face in silver-streaked gold tangles. A buckled leather portmanteau lay on its side near her feet.

Evelyn grasped at the front of her gown where her babe rested deep inside, innocently growing, lovingly anticipated. "M-Mother?"

Chapter 15

Evelyn's stunned mind scrambled to accept what her eyes were seeing.

Impossible.

She ignored the bedraggled woman for the moment and looked to her companion, a local farmer she vaguely recognized from being introduced to him at the Stage House's most recent supper dance.

He tipped his hat to her. "Ma'am, remember me? Ike Barnes. This here lady says she's your ma."

"Y-Yes," she managed hoarsely. Never had she considered a confrontation with either of her parents, not after their betrayal, the way they had denounced her.

She returned her perusal to the woman who'd brought her into the world. Mother looked awful, her usually immaculate appearance ruined by the hardship of her journey. Having traveled by train and then by stage to get here, Evelyn well understood what Winnifred Calhoun had endured for weeks on end.

An unwelcome thought occurred. "Where's Father?" Panic assailed her at the disapproval she knew would darken his stern, aristocratic face. Once he'd learned of the babe, what dregs of affection he deigned to show her had dried up like tumbleweed and blown away.

Even now, that knowledge was like a stab to the heart.

"I'm alone." Mother sniffled, blinking rapidly at the wetness clinging to her lashes. "Your father is divorcing me for another woman."

A low growl from Mister Barnes sounded suspiciously like a threat toward her father.

Evelyn gaped. "What? He can't do that!"

Of course he can, she self-chastised. Women had no rights at all, which meant Father could throw his wife in the streets with only the clothes on her back, nothing to be done about it.

The significance of her mother's solitary state suddenly struck her. "Am I to understand you traveled here on your own?" *Same as me,* she almost added.

Lips tight, her mother nodded. "He gave me a scant amount for the trip and told me not to come back."

Resurgent bitterness assailed Evelyn. Father had always been a cold, stern man, but this cruelty was beyond anything she'd thought even he was capable of.

Footsteps thudded behind her right before Addie wriggled past. The little girl's eyes widened, an adorable gasp falling from her mouth.

"Who are you? You look just like Missus Blackwood." Addie excitedly danced in place. "Are you her sister?" Grinning widely, she regarded Evelyn. "I got a little sister." Her smile fell. "She can be annoyin'."

Mother's expression lightened, as it did whenever someone made the comparison. "I'm her mother, sweetheart, but people sometimes mistake us for sisters."

Nate stepped up beside her, the pandowdy bowl still clutched to his chest. "Addie, come on." He nudged her onto the porch. "Ma said not to wear out our welcome."

He tipped his head at Ike Barnes in greeting, then flashed a quick smile toward her mother as he urged his cousin down the steps. "Nice to meet you, ma'am."

Handing off the bowl to Addie, he ran toward the horse and caught his halter, leading the docile animal to the buggy while she hollered, "Bye, ladies. Bye,

Mister Ike." Astonishingly, she managed to retain hold of the pandowdy.

As the children drove away, Mister Barnes spoke up. "Is there a place I can put your ma's things?"

Evelyn's good humor from the impromptu, fun visit evaporated when she eyed the portmanteau he had rescued from the ground. How had her life flipped so crazily in a matter of minutes?

With a sigh, she waved them both inside. "Please set it in the entry for now. Thank you."

Her mother ventured inside, her expression unreadable as she studied the walls and furnishings. Evelyn held in her temper, knowing she'd find the small ranch house lacking compared to the rich opulence of the Calhoun estate.

After Mister Barnes deposited the unwieldy trunk where she'd indicated, he bade them both goodbye. Other than a glance in his general direction, Mother offered nothing in the way of thanks for his escort in an unfamiliar, often dangerous region.

Evelyn vowed to do something nice for the man as atonement for such impoliteness.

Keeping her eyes downcast, her mother asked, "Might I freshen up?"

Struggling to remain calm, Evelyn showed her into the kitchen where Richard kept a fresh bucket of water on the counter, retrieving a clean linen for her to use. "I'll be in the next room when you're finished."

Stiffly, Evelyn reclaimed her sofa seat, fuming. Resentment toward the woman who'd sided with Father over giving an unborn child away—as if it were nothing!—gripped her hard and wouldn't let go.

Twenty minutes passed, and still Mother didn't join her. Just when she decided the woman was hiding out in the kitchen, too afraid to face the daughter she'd betrayed, her mother approached and delicately perched on the overstuffed chair near the fireplace.

"How did you find me?" Evelyn asked coolly, resting a hand protectively across her stomach.

Mother licked her lips, nervously plucking at her skirt. "When you never arrived at the nunnery, I made a few subtle inquiries."

An involuntary snort of derision escaped Evelyn's lips. "I can't imagine why you cared."

Flushing from neck to temple, her mother dropped her gaze to the floor. Sunken cheeks and visible exhaustion seemed to drag her down, until reluctant guilt clawed at Evelyn for not being more welcoming.

Forgiving her parents such abandonment could prove nigh impossible. This level of stress and upset couldn't possibly be good for the tiny life growing inside her, either.

Evelyn strove to swallow her pain. Yet an uncomfortable silence filled the room, stretching into minutes, until finally they both spoke at once.

"Are you hungry?" she began.

"Perhaps I should find a hotel in town," her mother stated baldly.

Exiting the Gambling Galleria, Richard straightened his Stetson, where it'd been knocked askew when he'd broken up a brawl. *Again.* With the menagerie museum still in town, a handful of its workers liked causing trouble in their free time. He intended to speak with the owner about keeping their people under control or moving on. As exciting as it was to have the show in town, the safety of Little Creede's townsfolk took precedence.

Since Sam Singleton spent most of his time in Rocky Gulch, overseeing the new casino, the Galleria patrons were often left to their own devices.

Halfway to the jailhouse, he spotted Ike Barnes striding toward him. Richard couldn't quite determine what the odd look on the man's face meant.

Now what?

His thoughts immediately flew to Evelyn, and his pace quickened as he hurried to meet Barnes. They both came to a stop near the milliner's. "Ike, is there a problem?"

The man scratched his stubbled jaw. "Well, there's somethin' all right. Your wife's ma showed up on the afternoon stagecoach. She looked mighty travel weary too."

Richard's brows arched in surprise. *Her mother?* That couldn't be right. As he understood it, from the little Evelyn shared with him, both her parents had disowned her when they discovered her condition.

"How do you know she's Evelyn's mother?"

"Wasn't hard to figure out." A quick grin flashed across Ike's face, followed by a low chuckle. "She looks just like your wife. I introduced myself and offered to find you, but she insisted she only wanted to see her daughter."

He gave Richard a sheepish look. "What could I do? I dropped her off at your ranch not more than twenty minutes ago."

Thinking back on his wife's despair over Horace Calhoun's decision to ship her off to a nunnery where she'd be forced to give up their babe, a jolt of anger blasted through Richard. A mother who condoned her husband's meanness toward their own child was no mother at all.

He pushed aside his fury. "How'd that go, when they saw each other?"

Ike's amusement faded. "Not very well, I'm afraid. Your wife didn't seem too pleased to see her."

"No, can't imagine she did."

"The mother looked to be in a bad way. I felt sorry for her."

Richard's protective instincts toward any woman who was in trouble smothered some of his annoyance. "I appreciate it, Ike."

"You're welcome, Deputy. Good luck." With a brief nod, Ike continued down the street.

In the jailhouse, Joshua Lang looked up from hanging wanted posters. "How'd it go at the Galleria?"

Richard frowned, coming to a stop near the sheriff's desk. "I'm thinking the menagerie is more trouble than it's worth. This is the third time this week I've had to warn the workers to calm it the hell down."

Lang plopped down into his chair. "I don't know, folks sure seem to be enjoying the shows. They're coming in from as far away as Leadville to attend. I'd say the owner's one happy fellow, finance-wise."

"Yeah, I sure understand financial solvency." Richard glanced out the dusty window as a group of rambunctious children tore down the street in the direction of the Galleria. "To be fair, it's the same small group of men each time."

"Have they hurt anyone?"

"No. They mostly drink too much and get loud. Obnoxious. Fight amongst themselves. Disturbs the poker players, and Knight's starting to get annoyed." He chuckled. "I'm afraid he might shoot one of 'em."

A flash of humor crossed Joshua's face. "With that tot of his running all over and making mischief, I don't think the man's getting much rest. Anything might annoy him. Except his wife and son, of course."

Richard recollected how the sizable man had been mellowed by his sweet, diminutive wife and a boy who was his spitting image. "Never seen a bigger man fall so fast."

"Careful there," Joshua joked. "Won't be long and you'll be a father yourself with a brand-new family. Then you'll understand."

"Suppose so." Lifting his hat, Richard scraped his fingers through his matted hair. "Speaking of family, I have a problem I need to deal with. I'll be gone the rest of the day."

"Nothing too serious, I hope."

"Not sure yet. Evelyn's mother arrived this afternoon and Ike took her out to the ranch. Said my wife was none too pleased to see her."

Little Creede being the small, nosy town it was, it hadn't taken long for everyone to know the history between him and his bride.

"Good luck. See ya in the morning."

"Thanks, Joshua."

Richard made good time getting back to the ranch. The sound of raised voices from inside had him quickly dismounting, ground-hitching Cloud, then bolting for the porch. He snagged the latch as an unfamiliar voice protested, "It's not that I agreed with your father, but he was my husband. I had no choice."

"There's always a choice." Evelyn's retort echoed through the open window.

"I'm sorry. I shouldn't have come."

Flinching at the deep sorrow in the woman's tone, more of Richard's exasperation toward her fell away. Sighing, he entered the ranch and approached the sitting room where Evelyn paced. Her mother, who bore a strong resemblance, older but still strikingly beautiful, sat in a chair looking miserable.

He strode over to Evelyn and wrapped a comforting arm around her shoulders. "I saw Ike in town, and he told me we had a guest."

Forcing a welcoming demeanor that he wasn't feeling, he addressed her mother. "I'm Richard, your daughter's husband."

She nodded. "Winnifred Calhoun." Her mouth trembled slightly before she firmed it in a bid to hold back the emotion glistening in her blue eyes, so similar to Evelyn's. "You must hate me. It was a mistake to come here."

She began to rise, but Richard stopped her with a staying gesture. "No. Please don't leave."

Evelyn might be upset with her mother, but family was family. If Missus Calhoun truly wanted to make amends, Richard wouldn't stand in the way. Hell, he'd help smooth things over with his wife if he could be convinced it was in her best interests.

"Is there a reason you've sought out your daughter?" He tried to keep his tone gentle, but he needed to know her intentions.

Guilt swamped him when her face paled. Two fat tears rolled down her cheeks, yet she straightened her spine, lifting her chin in the same manner as Evelyn did when she got ornery about something.

A smidgeon of admiration edged out some of his suspicion.

"I-I wanted to ask for Evelyn's forgiveness." Rapidly blinking away tears, her attention shifted to her daughter. "You might not believe me, but I'd already decided to leave your father to find you, before he turned me out."

Richard growled, "Your husband forced you from your home?"

She nodded solemnly. "He is divorcing me to marry another." She didn't appear to be overly upset about it. "I'd very much like to help during my daughter's confinement as well as the opportunity to know my grandchild."

The last words held a pleading tone as Winnifred stared at her hands, clenched together on her lap. Protective by nature, Richard held a soft spot for females and children, and this woman appeared to be someone who needed protecting.

Evelyn's rigid bearing didn't bode well for a reconciliation, at least not right this minute. He understood her enough to know if she didn't give her mother a chance to redeem herself, his soft-hearted bride would suffer with guilt the rest of her life.

Tucking her closer to his side, he swept loose strands of hair behind her ear. "What do you say? She can stay in Robert's old room for now. After the babe arrives, we can add on if everything works out." When her lips pinched in a stubborn line, he added softly, "She has no place else to go."

Winnifred spoke up in a hushed voice, the shadows under her eyes indicating her exhaustion. "Once I find employment, I can rent a room in town."

Finally, Richard spotted a bit of sympathy in Evelyn's expression. "We can discuss such things later. I'm sure you're tired after your long journey."

Her posture remained stiff as she moved away from him. "Richard, please show Mother to her room while I start dinner."

"Thank you, Evelyn," she murmured, almost too quietly to hear.

Richard held out his arm for her to take, as the poor woman looked ready to collapse. "Let's get you settled, Missus Calhoun."

Rising to her feet, she sent him a look of gratitude. "Please, call me Winnifred. And might I call you Richard?"

He patted her hand where it rested in the crook of his elbow. "Of course."

Chapter 16

Hidden by high brush and some spindly junipers, Grover and Floyd hitched their horses on a low branch.

"We ain't close enough," Floyd whined, tapping his holster with his usual impatience. "I say we go in over there." He jerked a thumb toward an open area fronting the cabin.

The mid-afternoon sun beat down on them. Dragging the back of his hand across his sweating forehead, Grover eyed him in disgust. "You think someone won't poke their head out a window and spot us? This ain't a social call. I hear Washburn's gotten feeble. Don't mean he can't shoot a gun."

His brother snorted. "He's only got the one leg. How's he gonna shoot with just a leg?"

Irritated, Grover gave him a hard shove, almost knocking him over. "Weren't you payin' attention the first time we came to talk to the miners? The old coot sits in one of them rollin' chairs. You think a man can't aim and shoot from a chair, dumbass?" He motioned to the path. "Let's go. Quiet-like."

They eased around several jutting rocks, following the rough path toward Clem Washburn's cabin. Bigger than the rest, it boasted extra rooms and a front porch instead of a crooked stoop. Grover found himself fingering his own pistol as he led the way.

The miners respected Washburn. He'd been around longer than most, one of the first men the Carter Mine hired on. He owned a large claim, pulling substantial ore from the earth. Up until a few weeks ago he'd brought all his minerals to the smelter for processing. When he'd backed out, several other miners followed.

Grover aimed to persuade Washburn into returning, whatever it took. If the smelter sank, they'd be in terrible trouble. Deadly trouble.

I'd be lucky to save my own hide, let alone my brother's.

Coming around on the only windowless side, Grover spotted a hunched over figure, sitting on a tree stump, whistling under his breath as he whittled.

It'd been some months since he'd seen Clem Washburn, but the man had aged, now completely gray and thin the way sickly folks were. One of his trouser legs had been folded and pinned above the knee. A single homemade crutch lay on the ground next to the tree stump. The chair he used most days sat empty on the porch.

The former miner looked pretty infirmed but looks could be deceiving. Motioning Floyd to the opposite side behind where Clem sat, Grover stealthily approached, waiting until the man noticed him.

With a muttered curse Clem tossed aside the piece of whittling and grasped his carving knife like a weapon. "Yer trespassin'."

"Now, Mister Washburn," Grover said, holding both hands out placatingly, "they's no call for that. I come by to ask why you stopped bringin' ore to the Shaw Smelter. Why, Floyd and me been missin' you." He glanced to the side where his brother loomed. "Ain't we, Floyd?"

Clem visibly paled as he turned, seeing for himself how close Floyd stood and the way he stroked the holster strapped to his leg, fingers hovering over the pearly handle of his fancy Remington. But the frown the man wore when he glared at Grover was anything but weak. "I already got processin' set up for my ore. I don't need yer cheatin' ways."

Floyd surged forward. "We ain't cheated nobody."

"*Floyd*, stand down," Grover bit out.

If his idjit brother ruined their chance to get the Carter miners back, he'd personally shoot him. As it was, only the memory of their mother's pleading eyes, as she choked through the final moments of her death, kept him from drawing on Floyd himself. He'd promised to look after his kin, and he wouldn't break that promise.

Grover took off his hat and held it over his heart. "Mister Washburn, we didn't cheat nobody. If they's a shortage, it was an accident, and we can fix it. But we can't do business without them minerals, you see? We got to have product to make silver, then we got the funds to pay you."

Clem half-raised from his seat, balancing on his good leg, still clutching the knife. "You shorted us, Shaw. More than once. I got nothin' else to say. You and yer brother ain't welcome here."

"We ain't leavin', Washburn." Grover spread his feet aggressively. If the fool needed some harder persuasion, he'd sure get it.

"Clem?" a soft voice queried from the shadows. A red-haired woman stepped off the porch.

"Go back in, Nellie." The man's voice wobbled with panic.

Washburn's wife, I'd bet. Grover tried to catch his brother's eye in case he did anything stupid, but as usual, the dummy reacted predictably.

She'd almost reached her husband's side when Floyd pounced, grabbing her around the waist, hauling her close. He whipped out his pistol and shoved it against her ear. "I got yer woman, Washburn," he rasped, sniffing at her neck while she struggled to break free. "She smells sweet."

Instantly Clem threw his knife aside and vaulted himself off the tree stump, rolling once. Before anyone could react, the gimpy miner came up on his only knee, a deadly-looking Colt pointed directly at Floyd's heart. "Let 'er go," he snarled.

"I ain't lettin' go." Floyd gripped Nellie tighter, shifting slightly as if to protect himself from flying bullets. "Gonna keep her 'til we get what we want."

Knowing his brother was crazy enough to shoot the woman, Grover opened his mouth to speak, when a rifle barrel rammed into the back of his head.

A deep voice growled, "Tell your brother to drop his gun and step away from my mother."

Judging by the breadth of the hard-muscled chest behind him, Grover wagered this new threat had a good half-head or more on him. He'd snuck up on them so stealthily, Floyd hadn't even seen a thing. There wasn't a chance to draw.

Outnumbered. For now.

"Floyd, drop the gun and let Missus Washburn go," he ordered, bringing his hands up in surrender.

"The hell I will," Floyd shouted, his attention split three ways as he tried to retain control of a standoff gone bad. His trigger finger visibly shook, while Clem's aim held steady and true, his eyes black with fury.

"Just do as I say," Grover roared, as the cocking of weapon hammers echoed in the still air, ready to go off if anyone breathed wrong.

For a moment he didn't think his wild-eyed brother would obey, but with a foul oath Floyd released the Washburn woman.

She ran for the porch as Clem carefully uncocked his Colt, rasping, "Now drop your gun."

"Do it, Floyd," Grover urged, feeling sweat trickle down his spine. "Lay it down and step back."

Floyd grumbled loudly under his breath but obeyed.

Grover felt his entire body sag in relief when the rifle muzzle eased off the back of his head. Then he tensed again as a heavy hand pushed him toward his brother. He stumbled, catching hold of Floyd's shoulder, turning to size up the Washburn kid who'd threatened him.

This was no kid. Towering in height and broad in shoulder, this was a grown man whose large fists could probably pound rock into powder. A thatch of black hair hung over one narrowed eye and he wore the rough, ore-stained clothing of a miner.

The man raised his rifle, his expression lethal. "I'll ease off the trigger as soon as you two ride out of here, so I suggest you collect your weapons and mount up. In case my finger slips." He bared his teeth in a mocking smile.

Before Floyd could say anything else and possibly condemn them both to death, Grover grabbed his arm. "Don't speak, fool."

Chapter 17

"Anyone here?" Richard called out, shutting the door to the coach station behind him. The stuffy little office hadn't changed since Abner Dale first took over several years ago as station master.

Richard gave the place a fast onceover. Other than a fly hanging precariously off a window ledge and a messy desk, the man kept the station spotless.

"Abner, you around?"

"Aye, hold your horses," came the muffled reply from a curtained-off area along the back wall.

Richard took out his bandana and mopped his face. "Hell. You need to open a few windows."

"Too much dust." The meticulous station master burst through the curtains, bespectacled eyes locking on the front door.

Richard heaved a sigh. "I shut it tight, Abner. Didn't let in a speck of dirt, I promise."

"Obliged to you." Abner made for the work table. "I suppose you'll be looking for this." He selected a sheet of telegram paper and held it out.

Richard handled it gingerly so as not to smudge the ink. "When did it come in?"

"Half hour ago. I sent Danny to let you know, but that boy's a scatterbrain. Like as not he ended up over at Loman's store, begging a cookie off Betsey."

"I expect so." Richard read over Abner's precise handwriting with mounting excitement.

Shaws wanted in Chicago. Suspected of murdering local judge. Pines family pulled their support. Please advise if more is needed.

"Is it what you were looking for, Deputy?" Abner queried, tugging a blindingly white handkerchief from his pocket to polish his spectacles.

Richard nodded, tucking the paper inside his vest pocket. "It is indeed, Abner. Thank you kindly."

Out on the stage platform, he formed his plans. With Joshua out at Rocky Gulch today, conferring with Sam Singleton at the new Galleria, he'd have Ben mind the jail. Edward Coogan could come with him as backup for bringing in the Shaws. The kid had been chomping at the bit to prove himself. In fact, the last time Ben got chosen for extra duty, Edward had protested being slighted.

A ride out to the smelter would give the young lawman a chance to experience deputizing, something Richard understood all too well.

With an official 'wanted' bounty on the Shaws' heads, he finally had the legal right to haul them in and ship them off to Silver Cache for their time in court.

He peered up at the late-afternoon sun. Most of the day was over. If he and Edward went to the smelter to deal with the Shaws, not only would they chance a dangerous situation, but they could be stuck out there for hours. Making an arrest in the dark wasn't a smart move.

Tomorrow, after the picnic.

No doubt the brothers would try to squirm their way out of an arrest, but it wouldn't work this time.

"I should look for a room soon," Evelyn's mother called out. Sitting on the sofa across from the hearth, she'd stayed busy knitting a blanket during the two weeks she'd been there. "You and Richard need your privacy. I don't want to be a burden."

Evelyn set aside the broom she'd been using to sweep the kitchen floor as embarrassment burned her cheeks. Hard as she tried to be quiet when Richard did those things to her body with his talented hands—*and mouth, for goodness' sake*—she knew their lovemaking was noisy.

Last night had been a prime example of just *how* noisy.

A feeling of guilt crawled up her spine. Mother had kept mostly to herself since her arrival, and Evelyn had been fine with that, avoiding her whenever possible. Which was hard to do in such a confined space.

The few times she'd ventured into the kitchen, she had stared helplessly while Evelyn cooked or baked. Only once had Mother tried to assist in meal preparation, resulting in the roast catching fire, six eggs breaking when she dropped the basket on the floor, and what would forever be known as The Great Potato Explosion.

Another time, it had taken Evelyn hours to rub out the candle wax on a side table after Mother tried to affix one of Richard's homemade tapers directly to the polished surface instead of inserting it into an available wall sconce or, more sensibly, lighting an oil lantern.

Winnifred Calhoun had probably never worked a lamp in her life. The woman was a household menace. As amusing as she'd found her mother's actions, the tension between them hadn't lessened at all.

We can't remain like this any longer.

Inhaling a fortifying breath, she entered the sitting room and crossed to the sofa, settling herself as her mother put aside her chore. A long, awkward moment of silence ensued.

Mother's face fell. "I'm sorry."

"We should talk," Evelyn said at the same time.

They both paused and, for the first time since her mother arrived, shared a moment of camaraderie.

"You first," Mother urged.

Evelyn gathered her thoughts, longing to understand the reasoning behind her mother's decisions, good or bad. "Please tell me why you agreed with Father to send me away."

"I'm not surprised this is your first question."
She released a heavy sigh. "It's not an easy tale, I'm
afraid."

Evelyn found scant sympathy for her distress. If
they were to put the past behind them, make amends,
she needed to understand how her own mother could
allow such an act. "We have all day." She managed a
faint smile. "Unless you plan on helping me with
dinner again."

"Oh, that." Mother looked miserably toward the
kitchen. "I am rather a disaster, aren't I?"

"Everything is fixable and womanly chores can
be learned. As I have done." She leaned closer,
redirecting that flickering gaze. "There are more
important things to repair in this house, don't you
think?"

"Yes, of course." Mother clasped her hands
together in her lap and straightened her shoulders.
"You have to understand, sweetheart. I grew up in a
different time. While women have some rights today,
when I was your age there were none."

Evelyn opened her mouth to scoff at the excuse,
but Mother cut her off. "Please, let me finish."

Clamping her lips tight to keep all her thoughts
inside, she managed to remain quiet.

"I never loved your father. It was an arranged
marriage, and I barely knew him when we wed."
Distress dimmed her eyes. "He was not a kind or
gentle man, but he never beat me. If I remained silent
and obedient, he mostly let me be."

Her expression took on a faraway look, as if
remembering the past. "The marriage bed was not a
pleasant experience, but one I endured for the sake of
giving him the son he wanted."

Sympathy slammed into Evelyn. How lucky she
was, to have married a decent man like Richard. Most
of her antagonism evaporating, she laid a comforting

hand over Mother's whitened knuckles. "I never knew."

Her stiff posture eased. "I never wanted you to. I only wanted you to be happy. Unfortunately, all your father wanted from me was a son. He was furious when I produced a daughter instead."

Evelyn recalled how Father had often bemoaned the fact she'd been born a girl. In his mind, the least she could do was secure a marriage beneficial to the family to make up for her shortcomings. His words had cut deep, even though she'd have agreed to almost anything to earn his approval.

"After your birth, it became clear I was barren, and he no longer had use for me." Visible relief crossed her mother's face. "He fulfilled his needs elsewhere and my life became easier. All I had to do was be a good wife in front of his friends and raise you to be a dutiful daughter."

As her eyes brimmed with emotion, she brushed at her damp cheeks. "My biggest regret. I should have championed you, but I was weak."

Earnestly, she continued, "I was never so proud than when you had the courage to fight for your child, no matter the cost. And I was ashamed at my own cowardice."

Evelyn began to cry, sliding along the sofa cushions to embrace her mother. "I'm sorry, so sorry I doubted your love for me."

Her mother dissolved into sobs, hugging her tightly. "No, I'm the one who's sorry, sweetheart. I swear, I'd already vowed to leave your father and find you, before he cast me out. That's not a lie."

"I believe you."

As they continued to hold each other, chattering disjointedly about the future, their tears washed away an ugly past and the hurts that went with it.

Finally, Evelyn drew away, retaining hold of her mother's chilled fingers. "Why don't we set aside talk of moving, and think of more enjoyable ventures? Like the family picnic tomorrow. You have yet to meet everyone, and a relaxing barbeque outside would be a perfect opportunity—"

"Barbeque? Picnic?" Mother wrinkled her nose, looking as if she'd rather have a tooth wrenched out.

Evelyn squeezed her mother's hands. "Meeting the Blackwoods and their extended families was so wonderfully comforting for me. These people care. They are not cold or unforgiving, but warm and welcoming. Which would you rather have as part of your new life?"

Indecision seemed a palpable burden on Mother's elegant frame. Evelyn swore she could almost feel it herself as she tried to reason with a woman who'd lived far too long within a stifling marriage that had come close to smothering her completely.

Evelyn brought Mother's hands to her stomach and held them there. "Give them a chance, for me? For the grandchild soon to be born."

A reluctant smile curved the future Granny Winnifred's lips as the babe kicked beneath her touch. "Oh, goodness," she whispered, wide eyed with wonder.

Pressing her advantage, Evelyn urged, "Say yes to the picnic, to meeting your new family. Please."

Nodding slowly, Mother replied, "I will. But what if they don't like me?"

"They'll like you plenty, trust me."

Chapter 18

Evelyn sighed happily as they exited the ranch. It was the perfect day for a family picnic, although a bit overcast. Vivian Lang was hosting the event at Lucinda and Dub's new home, which was nearly completed.

Richard held the pan of pandowdy she'd made that morning with one hand and with the other helped her and Mother into the wagon. Knowing of Addie and Nate's fondness for the dessert, she'd promised the little girl a fresh batch for the picnic.

After handing her the covered dish, Richard climbed into the wagon and picked up the reins to nudge the horses forward. His horse was tied to the back of the wagon, following along. He'd mentioned having to leave right after everyone finished eating in order to deal with an issue in town, and that Harrison would see them home.

Resting the pan on her lap, happiness bubbled up inside her. "I'm so looking forward to a tour of the new ranch. I heard Dub did a lot of the work himself."

"That he did. He's been working on it for over a year now with some family assistance. I know everyone's anxious to see it completed. Though the Stage House is nice, Granny needs a backyard where she can sit out and watch her grandchildren play."

"I sure hope the nice weather holds up." Evelyn nodded toward the horizon where gray clouds gathered. "Might be in for some rain, later on."

Next to her, Mother shifted nervously. "Do they—do they know I was a terrible mother?"

"Mother, that's not true." Evelyn smiled wryly. "Well, not exactly true." She gave her mother's arm a gentle squeeze. "Besides, it's all behind us now."

Richard cut in, "My family doesn't listen to rumors. Once they meet you, they'll understand you're exactly where you need to be."

Mother cast Richard an affectionate glance. "Thank you. I can't tell you how much your acceptance means to me."

"No thanks are necessary, Winnifred. We're happy you're here."

By the time they reached the new property, a whitewashed ranch house with brown trim and matching shutters, the sun hovered high overhead. A large yard surrounded the good-sized home, with lush green grass and abundant wildflowers scattered about, making it picture perfect. A cool breeze offered some relief to the summer heat.

"Looks like we're the last to arrive," Richard stated, climbing down to help them from the wagon.

"Looks that way," Evelyn began, only to be interrupted when Addie ran up to them.

"Hello." She jumped up and down excitedly. "Did you bring the pandowdy? Is that it?" She reached out for the pan. "I can carry it."

Catherine Carter joined them, laughing. "Adeline Marie, give our guests a chance to get settled before you start badgering them."

The child's lower lip stuck out. "I just wanted to help."

Evelyn didn't know Catherine as well as the other ladies, but the few times she'd met her, she'd been impressed with the woman's self-confidant demeanor. Things were certainly different out West, since not many women back east had the fortitude to run a business in a man's world. And by all accounts, The Miner Stage House was an extremely successful establishment.

Catherine turned toward Evelyn's mother. "Hello. I'm so glad you could come. The family's anxious to meet you."

Mother's smile dimmed, then she squared her shoulders, her posture taking on one of determination. "Thank you for inviting me."

"Why of course, you're family now." She waved them to follow. "C'mon. Everyone's around back."

As they followed Catherine, Evelyn handed the pan of dessert to the still pouting Addie. "Why don't you put this with the rest of the food, sweetheart?"

The girl's face brightened. Clutching the pan to her chest, she skipped ahead, yelling, "They're here!"

The roar of chattering voices stopped, and when they rounded the corner right after her, all eyes were directed their way. Mother's steps faltered for only a split second as the introductions began.

Linking her arm with Richard's, Evelyn whispered, "I think it will go well. I just hope your grandmother behaves herself."

Richard whispered back, "Not likely. But I have faith your mother will handle herself."

Evelyn sure hoped so.

Catherine finally stopped in front of Granny Nia, sitting on a hanging swing Dub had thoughtfully attached to the awning over the back porch, out of the direct sunlight.

"Granny Nia," Catherine began, "This is Evelyn's mother, Winnifred—"

With a derisive snort, those ancient, shrewd eyes landed on Mother. "I know who she is."

Evelyn's stomach clutched and it was as if the air itself held its breath, waiting for Granny to finish her thoughts.

"You're the woman who tried to give away my great-grandchild."

"Ma," Dub scolded, as the rest of the family groaned.

Expecting Mother to turn around and demand to be taken back to the ranch, Evelyn was caught unawares when her chin lifted and she retorted, "Actually, that was my bastard of a husband. Something we have in common, I hear."

This time amused chuckles broke out as Richard leaned down and whispered with obvious humor, "Told ya."

A wide grin split Granny Nia's face, and she patted the empty spot next to her. "Have a seat, then. We'll compare stories."

Thanks to overindulging in whiskey last evening, Grover and Floyd had gotten a late start riding out to the smelter.

The midday sun, hotter than hell, beat on them, making Grover's head pound. Floyd had already puked once on the trail.

A hundred yards or so from the smelter, Grover knew something wasn't right.

The air didn't sting with mineral-tinged smoke. This still and quiet, the clang of grinding ore crushers should have been loud.

Grover dug his heels into his horse's sides, making the animal leap forward.

Ain't right, ain't right.

He thundered down the uneven path, around the deep bend that led to the open front where the carts and mules were hitched. They weren't there. Not a single cart nor mule stood in the rough grasses. Grover barely waited to pull up on the reins before he swung free of the stirrups and jumped down, Floyd trailing behind.

Dashing through the entrance, he stopped short, panting hard, his disbelieving eyes taking in the utter desolation all around him. The bitter taste of betrayal coated his tongue.

The two remaining carts of rough ore were gone. What had been piled on the bedding platform was also gone, including a container of flux. Grover rushed to the water bins, already dreading what he'd find.

"Dammit to hell!" His curses rang in the cavernous, empty room.

Gone. Everything was gone, the bullion soaking in the bin and even the bar forms. Whirling unsteadily, Grover took in the treachery of those employees he and Floyd had retained.

A snarl rumbled from his chest. The overwhelming need for vengeance almost knocked him to his knees.

I'm gonna track down every one of them traitorin' thieves and slit their throats.

His thoughts raced to the Under the Pines family and his gut lurched painfully. They were in a world of hurt for sure, with no way to continue paying for the criminal organization's protection.

Floyd reached his side, bushy brows climbing to his receding hairline as he surveyed the mess all around. "We been robbed?"

"Yeah. Robbed. By our own workers." Grover fisted his hands until his ragged nails cut into his palms. "Took it all, even the flux. We got nothin'."

"Sumbitches." Floyd yanked off his hat and wiped his face on his sleeve. "We'd only been gone a couple days. How can a few puny no-accounts rob us blind an' carry it off? They'd need mules, carts." He paused, then grabbed Grover's arm. "You check the office?"

"Ah, hell, the safe!"

They both bolted for the office, finding it unlocked, the latch busted and hanging loose. Though the small room was in shadows, it was easy to spot the corner safe, its door wide open, its contents ransacked. A handful of ledgers and some empty burlap money bags were all that remained.

Grover sank to the floor.

Ruined.

Granted, there hadn't been a whole lot of money stashed here, but in their current straits they needed every penny they could scrabble together. If they didn't disappear, they'd soon be dead men.

A piece of folded paper fluttered on the floor near the desk. Grover eyed it balefully, recognizing the stamped letterhead from the Georgetown telegraph office. Somebody must've delivered it to the smelter while they were in town, and one of the workers read it.

Reaching for it, he smoothed it out, dreading what it'd say. His eyes flickered over the uneven print.

With a foul oath, he crumpled it up and flung it across the room. It landed an inch from where Floyd stood.

"What's that?" He toed it with his boot.

"Final call. They want their money for the bullion advance we asked for and never paid back." Wearily, Grover got to his feet. "We're outta time."

"We gotta leave town, brother." Floyd started to drag him from the office. "We got money at the ranch. We can go someplace else."

Fury swamped Grover so swiftly, he nearly leapt for his brother's throat. "You think they won't find us?" He caught hold of Floyd's dirty neck and shook him like a rat. "Smarten up, you dummy. What we got saved won't buy us safety."

"What're we gonna do?" Floyd's whining reached new levels as he hung in Grover's grip.

"Shut up and let me think." He shoved his brother away. Pacing, his mind scrabbled for any solution.

They couldn't stay in Little Creede, not now. Hiding out in Cottonwood Springs wasn't an option any longer. A week or two in Silver Cache might be doable, but their faces were known there, especially at the saloons where they'd both been tossed out for cheating at cards.

The sound of stomping hooves snapped him out of his mounting dilemma, and he motioned to Floyd. "Somebody's comin' up the trail."

Drawing his revolver, Grover sidled to the far wall, keeping to the deepest shadows. Across from him, Floyd had also drawn his weapon.

Past the gaping entrance, two riders pulled up, their mounts churning dust.

"Who is it?" Floyd whispered.

Grover squinted, edging out further. Then stiffened. "It's the law!"

"Looks like that storm's heading our way after all," Edward said. As if to reinforce his statement, the sound of thunder rolled across a rapidly darkening sky. Lightning followed, illuminating the smelter roof.

Richard grunted in disgust. He'd hoped the foul weather would hold off until they'd made the arrests and had the Shaws contained. "Be careful when we confront these cretins, Eddie. They may not be the brightest, but they're still murderers. A cornered animal can be a mighty dangerous thing."

He had confidence in the kid's abilities but Coogan was still wet behind the ears, his only experience patrolling the mostly safe streets of Little Creede with an occasional foray through the Galleria during poker tourneys. If the brothers decided to put up a fight, anything could happen.

As they approached, Richard's intuition whispered, *Danger*. It was far too quiet, the place appearing abandoned.

"Wonder where everyone is?" Edward mused aloud.

Pulling up on the reins, Richard brought Cloud to a halt before they reached the building. He held up a hand, indicating Edward should stop. "Something's off here."

He scanned the property. This time of day there should've been at least one cart and mule out front, yet the rough patch of ground where the animals usually grazed was unoccupied, the dry grasses overgrown. No smoke emerged from the roaster's chimney.

A feeling of being watched fell over him. Eyes narrowing, he studied the smelter. When a streak of lightning lit the sky, he caught the glint of a rifle shoved between a gaping hole in the rotting wood on the top floor of the rundown building.

"Down, kid," Richard yelled, kicking free of the stirrups and jumping from the saddle as a bullet whizzed by his head. Rolling into a crouch, he swept both Colts from their holsters and fired off double rounds. Another quick roll had him partially sheltered by a large boulder, where he sent three more bullets toward the shooter.

Edward took cover behind a water trough and returned fire. For the next few minutes, the sound of battle filled the air along with blasts of thunder as the rain let loose.

"Grover Shaw," Richard shouted, blinking water from his eyes, "you and your brother, Floyd Shaw, are under arrest for the murder of Judge Ezra Toomey in Chicago. Throw down your weapons and come out with your hands up."

Even as the words left his mouth, he knew the brothers would never give themselves up.

"Go to hell," came the curt reply, followed up by more gunfire from two different locations on the top floor.

Damp dirt kicked up off to Richard's left. *Gotcha,* he thought with grim satisfaction. Now he knew the general vicinity of both men. Since the building abutted High Hill Summit, the only passage out was back the way they came, so an escape route was cut off.

Edward had positioned himself closer to the smelter. Richard motioned to get his attention. Pointing to the entrance, he mouthed, "On the count of three," as the storm intensified. Hard gusts of wind sent the rain sideways, instantly soaking him clear through.

Dripping wet, Edward nodded his understanding, determination evident in every line of his body. The downpour and rumbling thunder might give them some cover when they stormed the building. They were easy targets if they stayed out in the open.

He held up a single finger to Edward, who nodded grimly. Raising his voice to be heard over the thunder, he shouted, "The only way you're leaving, boys, is in handcuffs. Or dead."

Without an answer this time, Richard continued counting down, reaching three.

Edward began shooting. Darting out from behind the horse trough, the kid ran toward the building in a staggered line to avoid getting hit by a bullet.

Richard sprinted after him. Providing the young deputy more cover, he sent off a series of gunshots toward where he estimated the Shaws were hiding.

Edward disappeared inside. Seconds later Richard followed. The deputy was already scouring the lower level for danger. Between the two of them, it didn't take long to determine the first floor was deserted.

"Follow me." Richard crept up the staircase, Edward right behind. Reaching the top, they both sidled inside, weapons up, expecting a volley of gunfire from the brothers.

Nothing happened.

Richard turned in a slow circle, searching for any movement.

"There." Coogan pointed toward a ladder leading to an opening in the blackened ceiling.

Richard raced over and started climbing. When they reached the roof, he motioned for Edward to go left, while he went right. Flinging himself through the opening onto the unstable shingles, he spotted Floyd, holding a rifle aimed directly at him.

Though Richard's first choice was to take suspected criminals alive, Floyd left him no other option. Taking aim, he shot Shaw in the upper arm. The impact sent the man sailing off the roof, followed by the sound of him bouncing off an overhang, before hitting the ground with a dull thud.

When Richard spun back around, his Colt raised to chest level, his gut clutched at the sight of the deputy lying unconscious, blood soaking the gaping roof boards beneath his back.

Grover Shaw stood over the kid, ready to put a bullet in his head.

"Don't do it," Richard growled, ready to blow Shaw's brains out if he made one wrong move.

Freezing, Grover glared furiously. "Looks like a standoff, Blackwood. You shoot me, I shoot him." A nasty smile spread across his face. "Floyd, get the man's gun."

Now it was Richard's turn to bare his teeth. "Your brother had an accident. Fell off the roof."

Grover's mouth tightened, fury distorting his scarred features. Keeping his weapon aimed at the deputy and his eyes locked on Richard, he edged toward the exit hatch. "Here's what's gonna happen, then. I'm leavin', and you're gonna stay and take care of your deputy. He's bleedin' bad. If you don't tend to his wound real soon, the boy'll bleed out."

Richard bit back his demand for a surrender, knowing Grover was right. He needed to get to Edward soon or he could die. Though it infuriated him to do so, he had no other choice but to let the

Shaws go. He'd take Edward to Doc Sheaton's, then put together a posse to hunt these two down.

He held his Colts steady. "Go on. Git!"

As Grover climbed the hatch and jumped out to the ground, Richard hurried to Edward's side.

Chapter 19

Rage exploded inside Grover as he reached his brother and saw his condition.

I'm gonna murder Blackwood with my bare hands.

He stared down at Floyd, one arm and both his legs sprawled in unnatural positions, surprised to see his chest still moving. The idjit might not be dead yet, but besides what appeared to be a bullet wound to his arm, the sizable shaft of wood sticking through the edge of his ribs would soon finish the job.

"Dammit," he gritted out, falling to his knees.

He doubted Blackwood would shoot him in the back. The man was a lawman with too much stupid honor for such an act. "I can't leave you here. Ma would come back from the grave and nag me for the rest of my life."

Ignoring the grief crushing his chest, he took off his shirt and tore it into strips. When he removed the wooden shaft, blood gushed out of his brother in thick streams. Fury locking his jaw, Grover managed to wrap the wound with the cloth.

Lifting Floyd into his arms he carefully placed him across the back of his horse, face down, before climbing on behind him. Leaving his brother's horse to graze, Grover rode away.

Not only was he losing his only living kin, but the business that had provided the funds necessary to make payments to the Pine's organization was gone. All because of Richard Blackwood.

Hate burned through Grover, hotter than the fires of hell. If it was the last thing he did, he'd make the man pay.

Twenty minutes later, the sound of his brother mumbling his name brought Grover to a fast stop. Dismounting, he lowered Floyd to the ground, keeping an arm braced under his back. Tears slid down Grover's face, which only made him hate Blackwood even more for causing weakness to unman him.

Aggravation toward his brother also rose up inside him at how the dumb cur had gone and got himself killed. With much effort, he managed to hold back the acid words on the tip of his tongue. He didn't want their last moments together to be rancorous.

Floyd's dazed eyes met his. "Grover?" He fumbled with his good arm, keeping his other hand over the wound on his ribs. Even bound with Grover's shirt, blood oozed through his fingers. "Wha' happened?"

For only the second time in his life—the first being when Ma died—Grover's thoughts were on the needs of another, instead of himself. Being minutes older than Floyd, it'd been Grover's vow to keep him safe.

I sure as shootin' failed. Sorry, Ma.

Floyd's brows drew down, glazed confusion evident in his eyes. "Why you cryin'?"

Sniffing hard, Grover shook his head, wiping snot from his nose with the back of his arm. "It's nothin', brother. Rest now."

Floyd peered at the place where he held his hand against his wound, and what little color he had in his face drained away. "What th'—" A sudden coughing spell wracked his body from head to toe, an agonized moan bursting from his lips.

Grover wrapped both arms around his brother to help stabilize the spasms. "Shh. You're gonna make it."

Once the coughing fit ceased, Floyd ground out, "Bullshit." His resolute gaze met Grover's. "I never heard you talk to me kindly. Must mean I'm dyin'."

"You're not dyin'!" A lie. There was no surviving an injury like this.

As the life faded from Floyd's eyes, his last words were gut wrenching. "I'll tell Ma you said hello."

Then he was gone, leaving Grover alone in the world.

Wiping sweat out of his burning eyes, Grover stood back from the makeshift grave and bowed his head.

It's all I can do for you, brother.

Wanting to leave some kind of meaningful marker, he'd shoved Floyd's pearl-handled Remington into the soft dirt. It slipped sideways, but he was beyond caring. Every pore on his overheated body, every nerve ending he possessed, all clamored for justice.

For vengeance.

Plotting pushed through Grover's need to mourn his twin's murder. Some things were more important than others. There'd be time to grieve. Right now, the urge to put a bullet through Blackwood's heart blotted out everything else. The moment Floyd died in his arms, Grover's task was set.

Kill Blackwood. Escape.

"Mexico," he muttered. The law couldn't touch him there. With substantial funds he'd set himself up like a king, buy a lavish *hacienda* somewhere, and find himself a sweet *senorita*. He'd live out the rest of his life knowing he'd not only gotten retribution for Floyd's murder but was safe from the Pines' family reach.

First, he'd need money. For that, he'd have to wait until the bank opened again.

A plan formulated in Grover's brain as he collected his horse. By his calculations it was Friday and the bank wouldn't be open for three days. In the

meantime, Grover recalled a few hidden, deserted
mines out a ways from Prairie Lick. He'd go there
and bide his time, make the law in Little Creede think
he'd run off.

Then, when things died down, he'd sneak into
town and rob the bank. With money in his saddlebags
he'd hightail it to Blackwood's ranch and avenge
Floyd. For the first time in many hours, a smile split
Grover's chapped lips.

Soon, you murderin' sumbitch.

Halfway between Rocky Gulch and Silver Cache,
Richard studied the freshly dug grave as the heavy
rain ran off the brim of his Stetson. Floyd's fancy
pistol had been pushed into the dirt mound, over
where the man's heart would be.

An angry growl rumbled from his throat. "The
storms washed away any good tracks."

After delivering Edward to Doc Sheaton, who'd
assured them the boy would make a full recovery,
they'd put together two separate posses to search for
the Shaws. Joshua had taken Frank and Harrison with
him, leaving Ben Parsons to man the jail in town.
Knight had joined Richard.

A welcomed surprise had been the appearance of
his brother, Robert, leading Buster who'd whinnied
and pushed against Richard's shoulder hard enough to
knock him back several feet. Relieved to be out on a
manhunt with his prized stallion instead of the
daintier Cloud, Richard mounted up and the
threesome had ridden out.

That'd been a full day and night ago. The rain
had started up again a few hours earlier and was now
a torrential downpour, the air overly warm and
muggy. His gaze shifted to the men standing to his
left. "Grover could be anywhere."

Robert clamped a bracing hand on his shoulder, sending water spraying from the soaked fabric. "I'm sorry, brother, but I think we need to head back."

Sympathy deepened his gaze. "You telegraphed the law in a hundred-mile radius, along with Territorial, that's the best you can do."

Frustrated, Richard snatched off his hat, allowing the rain to cool his overheated skin. Every instinct he possessed clamored at him to keep looking until he found the no-account bastard, but Robert was right. They weren't getting anywhere.

He scraped his fingers through his damp hair and expelled a ragged breath. "Yeah. Let's head back."

As they remounted, a streak of lightning lit the sky followed by a boom of thunder. The dramatic display mirrored Richard's stormy emotions as Buster shifted skittishly underneath him.

"Easy, boy," he murmured, patting the side of his neck. As much as he hated to give up the hunt, his responsibility lay with his wife and Little Creede, to return home and protect what was his. With a flick of the reins, he urged Buster forward, disappointment resting like a lead ball in his gut. "Let's go home," he said to his companions.

They rode in silence for several miles, while the wind and rain slapped at their backs. During a lull in the booming thunder, Gleason called over to him. "Ah hear yer bride's mama is looking fer employment."

Word sure gets around these days. Richard nodded. "She is."

"Well," the gambler rumbled, "Ah been meanin' to tell yew, Thaddeus is relocatin' to Rocky Gulch t' play in Sam's new galleria. If'n the lady kin play the piano, even a little, I might jest have a job fer her."

Chapter 20

A huge smile broke over Evelyn's face at the tinkling notes coming from the Galleria's main salon.

Next to her, Nate Lang commented, "Your ma sure can play."

"Yes, indeed."

When Richard told Mother about the opening at Gleason's Galleria, she'd immediately traveled to town to show Knight her proficiency with the keyboard and had been hired on the spot.

Taking his proffered arm, Evelyn stepped forward. Ungainly in her eighth month of confinement, she counted herself fortunate he'd readied the buggy and given her a ride to the Galleria. "I do appreciate your assistance, Nate. Mister Blackwood would've had to stop in the middle of the day and come to get me, otherwise." She winked. "Or I'd be walking in the heat."

He blushed. "You know I wouldn't have let that happen, Missus Evelyn." He paused at one of the lobby sofas. "You should sit down."

"Let's go into the salon first. I haven't heard my mother play in a very long time."

They stood in the wide doorway, listening, as Evelyn's mother flowed from a rousing reel into the softer, sweeter notes of "Juney Lee."

"This one was always a favorite of mine." Evelyn hummed along.

"Naye, Naye!" The high chant came from behind them, as Alexander Gleason barreled into Nate's legs, chubby arms encircling his knees. Having met the exuberant, red-haired child once already, Evelyn laughed as the determined tot dragged her erstwhile escort into the salon and started dancing around him.

Evelyn's mother, spotting her audience, obligingly kept playing, adding her melodious voice to the lilting tune.

"Ne'er was there a purtier gal than my own Juney Lee,

I'll place a ring upon her hand, for soon she'll marry me."

Nate gave up standing still, catching Alexander under his arms to swing him to and fro, the boy's excited shrieks mingling with the song.

"No longer ere I'll roam alone o'er land or o'er sea,

But live in love with babes and hearth, beside my Juney Lee."

Knight Gleason came over, grinning as widely as his son. "Mah boy's a handful, ain't he?"

Evelyn turned to beam at him. "He's such a beautiful child."

She'd grown to admire the big, brash former riverboat gambler. He'd not only welcomed her to town but had given her mother a sumptuous room here at the Galleria, her meals provided and her every need met. For Winnifred Calhoun, this sort of respect was priceless. "I wanted to thank you for everything you have done for my mother."

"Yer mama's a real special lady. Why, the folks heah at the Galleria already love her. Ah hope yew know she kin stay heah as long as she wants, Missus Evelyn."

Knight patted her shoulder. "Now, ah understand yew ladies have places to go. Yew stop by the front desk first, so yer mama can collect her pay." He winked. "Tell her to buy herself somethin' purty."

"I will." Evelyn watched as he strode into the salon and scooped up his son in one brawny arm, tickling the boy amid fresh giggles.

Nate wandered over to her side. "I can drive you ladies wherever you want to go. My ma said I should."

"Oh, that's very sweet of you both. My mother might enjoy a visit to the mercantile and then the bank to set up an account. We'd love a ride." Evelyn allowed him to lead her back into the lobby and settle her into a chair, touched at his solicitous behavior.

While she waited for her mother to join her, Nate kept her entertained with stories about his brother's antics. Young Isiah was sweet but becoming quite a handful, as she'd seen for herself during her visit to Vivian's house this morning.

"Ma says if she ever finds herself expecting again, it'd better be a girl," Nate confided. "I think I'd kind of like that too."

"You're a wonderful older brother," Evelyn declared, earning another blush from the handsome teen. "And it was so much fun to see you with young Alexander."

She was spared from embarrassing him further by the appearance of her mother, pulling on a pair of intricately embroidered gloves, her hat already pinned to her upswept hair. Spotting Nate, she exclaimed, "I hope I haven't kept anyone waiting long."

"Not at all, ma'am." He stood, extending a hand to help Evelyn from her seat, then offered his free arm to her mother. When he adjusted his long-legged pace to their much-shorter steps, Evelyn could have hugged him.

After collecting Mother's pay, Nate bade them wait in the shade of the front porch while he pulled up the buggy's canopy. She and her mother settled themselves on the wide seat, Nate climbing in after to take up the reins.

A breeze tossed Evelyn's hair into her eyes. She cleared it away in time to spot Mister Prescott striding down the boardwalk.

At her excited hail, he looked up, a smile creasing his wrinkled face. "Hello, missy! I heard you recently married your young deputy. Good on you."

Evelyn flushed with pleasure. "Thank you, Tommy."

"You and your man have my best wishes." With a tip of his hat, he continued on his way.

"Who was that?" Mother inquired.

"A very sweet gentleman who took me under his wing when I traveled by coach to town, months ago."

Evelyn thought fondly of the elderly passenger who shared his provisions with her. Tommy's lively conversation had taken her mind off her troubles on the uncomfortable stage journey from Georgetown to Little Creede.

"I will have to thank him, since he attended to you. Perhaps we can ask him to supper," Mother suggested, as several passersby waved to her.

She waved back gaily, a surprisingly warm response.

Why, she's happy.

Sudden emotion stung at the back of Evelyn's eyes. She blinked rapidly to clear it away, noting they were already at the mercantile.

Nate jumped down to assist them from the buggy. "I'll wait for you," he began, but Evelyn shook her head. "I don't mind, Missus Blackwood."

She smiled at the boy. "I know you don't, but we'll be fine. It's only a few buildings down from here to the bank, and afterward my husband will meet us for lunch."

"If you're sure." Nate delighted both of them by sweeping into a creditable bow. "Ladies, enjoy your day." He clambered back into the buggy seat and took up the reins.

"What a courtly young man," Mother commented.

"He truly is." Evelyn gestured to the mercantile door. "After you, Granny." Her teasing remark got a laughing response.

Keeping to the alley trail, Grover crept toward the bank, dodging an outside privy on the way. It stunk to high heaven, adding to his already agitated stomach. Nerves, anticipation, and eating nothing but squirrels and a few rabbits these past days hadn't helped any, either.

I'll be eatin' good, soon's I get the money.

He'd laid low outside of Prairie Lick for longer than he'd intended, unwilling to fight the storms that'd passed through and turned the trails to thick slop.

Keeping a fire going in one of the smaller, deserted mines where nobody would see the smoke or think to look for him, Grover had plotted his future. For once his plans would be executed with cold logic instead of hotheaded impulsiveness. The extra time in the shaft, subsisting on what menial game he could find, afforded him additional focus.

He considered the location of the bank. Because the building sat on a corner, he could use that to his advantage. The boardwalk ended short of the front door. He'd never seen anyone approach from the dirt path.

Ignoring the sweat stinging his eyes, Grover studied his surroundings in all directions. This time of day most folks were inside eating their midday meal, leaving the street all but empty. *Now's my chance.* Sidling close to the bank's rough-hewn outer wall, he finessed the front door, opening it only enough to squeeze through. Immediately he dropped low, peering around the edge.

Nobody was inside except a single teller, a skinny, balding fellow wearing a bowtie. Grover sized him up and figured he'd be too lily-livered to offer any trouble when faced with a gun.

There was a dented spittoon sitting on the floor. Grover used it to wedge the door shut. It'd hold for now, and he'd escape through the back to the alley.

Drawing his revolver and holding it behind him, he strode to the window, waiting until the man looked up and noticed him.

The teller offered a smile, revealing crooked, stained teeth. "Morning, sir. How can I assist you today?"

Grover swung the weapon around and leveled it. "You can start by emptyin' the safe."

The teller's pale eyebrows rose as his Adam's apple bobbed. "I don't have the combination."

"Now, I don't believe that for a minute," Grover retorted. "I think you do. And if you value your life, you'll remember it right now."

The teller raised his hands. "There's no need for violence."

"Hurry up. I ain't got all day." Grover turned slightly and eyed the front. Any minute someone on the street could try to come in.

The sound of a cocked hammer jerked his attention around. Grover discovered the sawed-off muzzle of a double-barrel shotgun greeting him, chest-level. Too late he realized he should have pulled the hammer back on his own weapon.

"Put your gun away." The scrawny teller might look weak, but his voice was suddenly deep, his eyes hard and shrewd.

Grover looked down at the rifle an inch from his chest, held in a steady grip, cocked and ready.

I don't stand a chance in hell of getting in a shot first.

Slowly, he lowered and re-holstered his revolver.

"Now get out of here. Don't come back," the teller snapped. He prodded Grover with the rifle muzzle. "I ever see you again in my bank, I'll shoot."

With no other choice, Grover made for the back door.

"What a lovely couple the Lomans are," Mother said, holding the door for Evelyn to exit.

"They are." She took her mother's offered arm as they strolled down the uneven boardwalk. "They really liked you."

"Do you think so?" She paused, brushing at the sleeve of her gown. "I feel so untidy. Perhaps I should have worn my watered silk, except it's terribly wrinkled."

"Mother, stop that." Evelyn caught the fluttering, gloved fingers before they could hunt for imaginary dust. "You always look lovely. What you wear has nothing to do with it. If you remain beautiful here"—she pressed her mother's hand against her own heart—"then your clothes will only enhance it."

"When did you get so smart?"

Impulsively, Evelyn leaned in and kissed her cheek. "Some of it I learned from my husband. The rest, I learned from you." She urged her mother forward. "Now, let's continue on before Mister Gable closes the bank and runs out for lunch."

The sound of feminine laughter drew Grover to the mouth of the alley between the line of shops and the bank. He'd crouched in the shade, unable to reach his horse, berating himself for his stupidity in tethering the beast out front in the first place. He'd been afraid if he'd left it ground-hitched on the back path, the ornery stallion would've taken off.

The death of his brother had affected his focus. Steel straightened his spine. *Smarten up,* he silently berated. If he wanted revenge for Floyd, he needed a foolproof escape out of town, and fast.

Folks had begun emerging from various establishments. The street wasn't crowded yet, but it soon would be. His chances to kill the deputy dwindled with each minute, reinforcing his decision to ride out to the bastard's ranch tonight and shoot him there.

Kill the woman too. And that brat she's carryin'.

He eyed the hitching post where his horse stood, shaking off the flies buzzing around his ears. Across the street a few men loitered near the smithy shop, reminding Grover he had unfinished business with the owner, Jaworski.

No loose ends. Hadn't that order been drilled into his head—Floyd's, too—during the years they'd spent working for Under the Pines?

Now he had loose ends, and no foolproof opportunity to tie them up.

The laughter came again, closer. He peered around the building to see Blackwood's wife, walking along with another, older woman.

Grover'd made an oath to cause Floyd's killer unending pain, figuring the best way to hurt the man was to kill his wife and unborn child right in front of him.

But here was a better opportunity, and he wouldn't have to wait until tonight. He'd show the bastard a mother lode of agony, first.

Eye for an eye.

There wasn't time to ponder it further. Grover strode into the women's path and grabbed Blackwood's wife. Not giving either a chance to react, he shot the older biddy.

She dropped like a stone on the walkway.

"Mother!"

Struggling to break free, his hostage tried to kick him. "Let me go!" she screeched.

"Shut up." Grover swung her body against his, back to front, and shoved the revolver muzzle under her chin. "You're comin' with me."

Leaving one woman bleeding on the ground, he dragged his enemy's wife to his horse and awkwardly shoved her onto the saddle, climbing up behind her.

Chapter 21

"This is the second time I've been called to the Menagerie because you were causing a ruckus." Richard scowled at the teenage boys whose father, Boone Crawford, mined for the Carters. "Next time, I'll be talking to your pa."

All three boys mumbled, "I'm sorry." Both apology and pleading shone in their wide eyes at the thought of their father being called away from work due to their misbehavior.

Not that the man would ever raise a hand against them. Boone was an honorable man of integrity, and he expected no less from his large brood. With eight sons and three daughters, it was a wonder Richard didn't get called in more often.

"We're really sorry, Mister Blackwood," the eldest boy said, glaring at his younger brothers. "I told them to stop horsin' around but they didn't listen."

This was the last day for the museum and oddities exhibition, the workers busy tearing everything down. Due to the rainstorms that'd blown through the area over the past week, excessive mud made the job more difficult. Today wouldn't be any better, the smell of another storm in the air.

Richard was past ready for the Menagerie to move on. Biting back a chuckle, he maintained a stern frown. "What would your ma say about such conduct, I wonder?"

The troublemakers shuffled their feet, mumbling additional apologies and looking like they'd rather be anyplace than there, getting a scolding from the law.

Over the boys' heads, he spotted Ben galloping toward him. "All right, get out of here."

The three took off running as Ben drew near. At the hard look on his face, inexplicable unease cut through him. "Something wrong?"

Dismounting, Ben strode to his side and gripped his shoulder. "I'm sorry, there's no easy way to tell you. Evelyn's been taken by Grover Shaw. Her ma was shot."

White-hot rage blurred Richard's vision, followed up by a fear so strong his legs trembled beneath him. He inhaled deeply, steadying himself. "When?"

"Not more'n twenty minutes ago."

"Winnifred?"

"She caught a bullet in the shoulder, but fortunately it went clean through. Doc's patching her up now. Joshua's rounding up a posse. We should be able to head out within the hour."

"I can't wait." Richard grabbed Buster's reins. "You can catch up with me."

Ben gave a short nod. "I'm riding out to the Carter mine for Frank. We'll need his tracking skills." He nudged his horse forward, avoiding the activity of the Menagerie crew and local gawkers.

Richard studied the dark rolling clouds overhead, signaling more rain and storming, as if they hadn't already endured plenty. The brief, sunny respite they'd welcomed this morning wouldn't be nearly enough to dry up the trails, which might not work in their favor. Any new tracks could be washed away.

"Dammit," he muttered. Urgency beating down on him, he shoved a boot into the stirrup as Madame Zoee and her man—Harvey, he recalled—hurriedly approached. The woman's worried voice reached out to him. "Please, I can help."

Stifling a growl of impatience, he dropped back to the ground. With the need to get to Evelyn stabbing at him, Richard didn't have a moment to lose.

Madame Zoee placed her hand on his arm, her gentle voice imploring. "*Monsieur* Richard, I heard *le jeune homme*. Your deputy, yes?"

"Ma'am, I don't have time for this," he muttered.

"My woman knows things, sir," Harvey interjected. "Believe me when I say you can trust her."

Remembering Evelyn's friendship with the fortune-teller, he relented. "Make it quick."

"There were things I did not share with *Bebe* when I read her future. *Avec un enfant*, it makes her delicate, *non?* But I saw strange dirt hills near rocks. A shape like *l'ours*." Her hands formed into claws. "A bear, you see? I sense great danger for her."

Richard knew of the spot, Indian burial mounds nestled halfway to the first summit of Upper Bountiful Mountain. Offering the fortune-teller his thanks, he started to mount up but she grabbed his arm again.

"Please, she is special to me. You will contact me when you find her, *oui?*"

He paused, aching to leave yet understanding Madame's emotional state since it echoed his own. "Where can I find you?"

Harvey stepped forward and offered a slip of paper. "We return to our home in Baton Rouge for the rest of the year. You can telegraph us."

Nodding, Richard tucked the paper away. "I promise I will."

Climbing into the saddle, he urged Buster toward town.

The woman had to be wrong. There was no good reason for Grover to take Evelyn to Bear Rock Cemetery. Originally a shelter for a number of Cheyenne, when smallpox hit the tribe they'd buried their sick there before moving on. It now stood abandoned, a landmark between Little Creede and Prairie Lick, a good thirty miles north. With only a narrow passage, most folks avoided the area due to the nearly impassable terrain that cut through the rocky bluffs.

Did the man plan on hiding out from the law until things settled down?

Making record time to Sheaton's office, Richard leapt from the saddle and rushed in, finding Winnifred awake but in obvious pain as her wound was dressed.

Spying him, she jumped off the table, leaving Doc grumbling and holding a length of linen bandage.

"Richard!" She moved to his side on unsteady feet, stark fear evident in her tear-glazed eyes. Blood seeped through the unfinished bandage.

"Let the doc tend to you now," he gently admonished.

"Oh my God, he took her."

"I know." Mindful of her injury, Richard embraced her as she trembled. "I'll get her back, I promise."

He met Sheaton's somber regard. "How's she doing?"

"She should heal quickly, but I'd like to keep her for a couple days to be sure there's no infection."

Doc paused in trimming more linen. "Coogan came for his grandson and took him out to the ranch."

"Glad to hear it." Richard grasped Winnifred's shoulders and encouraged her to sit on the table. "I'm going to find Evelyn," he promised.

Winnifred nodded, tears rolling down her cheeks. "Please bring her home."

"I'm heading out now."

He turned to Sheaton. "Doc, Joshua's getting together a posse. Can you ride out with them? My wife might need you."

"Give me fifteen minutes to finish up here and I'll go with you."

"I can't wait." Richard strode to the door.

"Hold on." Doc retrieved a ball of twine and a slender knife from a drawer. "In case your missus is in labor, you'll need these. For the cord. You tie off in two places about three fingers apart, then cut between. You understand?"

"Yeah. Thanks."

Richard's lips thinned as he accepted the supplies, picturing his sweet wife forced to deliver her child without medical assistance, in the presence of a dangerous criminal.

Outside, he mounted up and rode to the spot near the bank where Evelyn had been taken. Due to the Menagerie still being in town, street travel had been unusually heavy, making it difficult to search through the hoof prints. Then he spotted several tracks leading into the pathway between the bank and a wide alley the locals often took out of town, toward Prairie Lick.

Praying he was right, Richard prodded Buster and the big stallion obeyed, breaking into a full-out gallop.

Needing a cool head, he fought down his panic. Every second that passed took Evelyn further away from him.

An hour later, he admitted to himself the fortune-teller could have been right. The tracks he'd singled out were heading toward the natural fork for Bear Rock Cemetery. Which made no sense at all, since there were easier escape routes.

What does Shaw have planned? Richard's fear for his wife intensified.

He urged Buster faster.

They'd been riding for what seemed like hours, and as hard as Evelyn tried to remain upright, she'd finally been forced to lean against the man at her back. His evil chuckle sent a chill through her.

"I don't bite," he murmured. His arms encased her, one resting on the saddle horn, the other gripping the reins. His foul breath blew across the side of her face as he whispered in her ear, "Much."

Nausea twisted inside her. The late-afternoon heat, oppressively stifling, broke her out in a miserable sweat that trickled into her eyes and dripped off her quivering chin. The amusement in his voice indicated he enjoyed her discomfort.

Her fright.

What did he want? Why had he taken her?

Evelyn had recognized him as one of the men who'd accosted her at the menagerie. After the second time she tried to ask questions, he'd slapped her hard and growled, "Shut your mouth."

He shot Mother.

Was she even alive? The anguish Evelyn had felt at seeing her lying unmoving in the street remained fresh in her mind. Overwhelming grief tightened her muscles until the ache became unbearable. The memory of her mother's collapse played in her mind with each punishing bounce of the horse beneath her sore, exhausted body.

For all their differences, if her mother died it would break Evelyn's heart. These past few weeks had been a balm to them both as they relearned each other outside of Father's cruel presence, and she very much liked the woman Winnifred Calhoun was becoming. How agonizing to lose her now, when she finally had a chance at real happiness.

Weeping silently, Evelyn struggled to protect her unborn babe, keeping her arms crossed over her protruding belly. On top of being scared and tired, the last half hour she'd suffered light pains radiating in her abdomen. Such a rough ride could cause the babe to come too soon.

They'd been traveling through a rocky ravine, with the horse steadily climbing a gentle slope. Short bursts of rain had lent a reprieve from the oppressive heat. Clearing a bend, she stared bleary-eyed at a wide open space near the foot of the mountain. Dirt mounds dotted the landscape.

Burial mounds, she realized with fresh horror.

Images of this man murdering her, leaving her body here where Richard would never find her, shot such agony through Evelyn she sobbed aloud.

"Stop your caterwaulin'." Reining to an abrupt halt, he snagged the back of her dress and shoved her off the horse.

With a frightened gasp, Evelyn clung to the side of the saddle and stopped herself from slamming head-first onto the rocky ground. Her legs gave out and she landed on her hands and knees, scratching her palms on sharp pebbles.

Dismounting, her tormentor fisted her hair, yanking her upright, hatred consuming his scarred face as he glowered at her. Terrified, shaking from head to toe, she barely managed to stand. Fresh tears brimmed her burning eyes and poured over her bruised cheeks.

Although Father had often been hateful with words and tone, he'd never harmed her physically. The violence this man heaped on her was both shocking and horrific, leaving her struggling to understand his actions.

He dragged her close until his bulbous nose touched hers. "You remember me?"

Her stomach roiled at the sour stench of body odor and chewing tobacco. "Y-You're the man from Madame Zoee's tent."

"The fortune-teller, yeah. You know why you're here?" he snarled.

Mutely, she shook her head.

"I'm Grover Shaw, and your man killed my brother. So now I'm gonna take somethin' from him."

He shoved her away, causing her to stumble weakly. His furious stare locked on her, he slid his gun from its holster. "I thought about keepin' you for myself and gettin' rid of the brat, but I can move quicker without you."

Dear God, no. Bile clogged her throat.

He shrugged. "It's better this way. Blackwood won't never find your body way out here." A broad smile broke across his face, in stark contrast to the evil in his eyes. "He'll spend the rest of his life wonderin' what happened to you."

With those final words, he pointed the pistol at her head.

At that moment, the babe kicked with what must have been both feet. Evelyn cried out. Tears blurred her vision as she lovingly caressed the spot where her child rested inside her.

"Shh, little one. Everything's going to be all right," she sobbed.

Regret tore at her. Richard would never have the chance to know his child.

Her husband was nothing like Horace Calhoun. Richard would have loved the babe as fiercely as she did, whether a boy or a girl.

When she raised her face, Shaw wore an odd expression. "Ma used to call Floyd her *little one* since he'd been so scrawny," he muttered quietly, almost to himself. Then his hate filled eyes landed back on her. "Until Blackwood killed him."

He cocked the pistol. Evelyn slammed her lids shut, bracing for the shot. Would it hurt or would she die instantly? It took every bit of fading strength in her body to remain standing.

A vicious pain in her womb forced a scream from her raw throat. The sudden rush of water drenched her skirts and she fell to her knees.

"What the hell?" Grover Shaw snapped.

Evelyn opened her eyes and found him watching her with disgust, his weapon hand lowered at his side.

"It's the babe. It's coming," she gritted out through clenched teeth.

"I don't give a tinker's damn." He shoved the barrel against her forehead hard enough to leave a mark.

Fury heated her blood. *Don't let him win.* Stiffening her spine, she held his penetrating stare. Silence stretched between them for endless moments as her life, and that of her child, hung in the balance.

Finally, he slammed his gun into its holster. "Ain't wastin' a bullet. You'll be dead in a few hours anyway." He barked a laugh that sounded forced. "Unless a wild animal gets to you first."

He remounted his horse, urging the beast forward until its massive hooves churned up the dirt a scant few inches from her body. Evelyn scrambled sideways, curling into a ball to protect her belly.

He smirked cruelly. "You and that kid's gonna make mighty tasty snacks."

Evelyn's shoulders sagged with relief as he galloped out of the clearing.

I still have a chance if I can stay alive long enough for Richard to find me.

Rising to her knees, her entire focus stayed on Shaw's image as it grew smaller and smaller, finally disappearing from sight. Only then did she squeeze her eyes shut.

Please find me, Richard.

Sudden, incapacitating agony pierced low in her abdomen. She clutched her stomach, moaning. The pain seemed to go on forever, before finally easing. Panting, she lay there until she was able to catch her breath, before attempting to sit up.

She scraped her tangled hair over one shoulder, licking her parched lips as she studied her surroundings, searching for a safer spot, finding nothing but rocks and burial mounds covering the landscape, an occasional low spot forming a puddle.

Her stomach rumbled with hunger. *Water too dirty to drink and no food.*

Heartbreak robbed her of hope when she realized her contractions would start up again and she'd be helpless to stop the babe from coming. She'd be all alone, vulnerable when night fell and the animals came out.

Forcing back a sob, all she could do was pray.

Chapter 22

Richard lifted each of his horse's legs in turn, examining his hooves and shoes for any damage as thunder rolled overhead. The stallion snorted, then nosed him in the back.

"Easy, boy," he crooned.

Relieved at finding no injuries or cuts, he peered upward toward the next section of Bear Rock and expelled a frustrated oath as sweat dripped down his face from the stifling humidity.

He'd ridden along the lower ridge most of the way, with occasional light sprinkles cooling him off. Soon he'd have to climb. The Cheyenne had buried their dead further up, where the summit opened into a small pasture and the ground held some moisture. Once he reached that spot, he'd have to walk, leading Buster to avoid damage to his fetlocks.

Discovering a small stream earlier had been a godsend. He'd been able to fill both of his canteens while his boy enjoyed a lengthy drink.

Shaw's up there somewhere.

Worry for his wife, not knowing what Grover was putting her through, ate at Richard until he thought he might lose his mind. The bastard would pay for every heinous crime he'd committed.

According to Winnifred, Shaw had whipped out the gun, had shot without even a second of hesitation. Somebody that evil would have no qualms or remorse over killing an innocent woman like Evelyn.

A true lawman strove to understand both sides; what drove a man to do wrong in the first place, or what made him resort to murder. Fury obliterated any thoughts of offering Shaw charitable understanding, given the fact he'd kidnapped Evelyn.

The man's time in Chicago under the thumb of a prominent and influential crime organization notwithstanding, his remaining years would be spent in prison.

Spotting the higher trail at last, Richard knew he wasn't far from the Cheyenne burial mounds. He stopped briefly to check Buster's hooves once more, then assured himself both Colts in his holster were fully loaded.

"Let's go, boy."

Leaving Blackwood's wife behind had been strangely satisfying, though Grover'd found himself unable to shoot her, given her delicate condition. Keeping his memories of Floyd uppermost in his mind, he'd banished most of the weak emotion when he left her for the animals to finish off.

Yet a twinge of misgiving lingered as Grover urged his horse down the trail toward the lower ridge. Which he doggedly ignored.

A light breeze dried the sweat on his neck. It'd get cooler as it got darker, until wind whistled through the rocks and boulders. Critters would come out to feed, some small, others bigger, more dangerous. When the woman gave birth there'd be blood. The smell would draw predators.

Even if Blackwood figures out where she is, he'll never get to her in time. His hatred for the man had Grover smiling for the first time since his brother's death.

A whinny, coming from a distance, jerked his attention back to his surroundings. Dismounting, he cast about for a hiding place. Nobody came up here anymore, one reason he'd chosen it. Maybe a riding party got lost or turned around on the north trail.

Or maybe Blackwood was pretty smart, after all.

Stashing his horse behind a clump of high grass, Grover crept forward, stepping carefully over loose stones, easing his revolver from its holster.

Being as he was the last living Shaw, his plan to kill the lawman escalated into hard desperation. "Come on, you sumbitch."

Stumbling forward, Evelyn moaned as another contraction hit her, low in the back. Weary, thirsty, aching all over, she somehow managed to remain on her feet. As dusk darkened the sky, all around her the ridge was coming to life.

The cacophony of howls, squeaks, and coyotes calling to each other rent the air. Unwilling to admit to herself how terrified she felt, she'd kept moving, frantic to locate a safe place. The skies opened up again, and she greedily opened her mouth in an attempt to quench her thirst.

Judging by the frequency of her labor pains, the babe wouldn't wait much longer to be born. She needed protection from the increasing chill as evening approached. Having given up on any lingering expectation of rescue, it'd become obvious she would deliver this child by herself.

What would happen after, she had no way of predicting. Alone in the dark with a newborn, she'd be utterly defenseless, not to mention terrified out of her mind.

The contraction eased, affording her a moment to inhale and exhale deeply. She had trekked alongside the burial mounds, shivering to think of what lay beneath each oval shaped dirt hill. Higher beyond, she had seen what appeared to be a small cave blocked on one side by boulders. Setting her sights in that direction, she trudged on, striving not to stumble on the loose stones under her feet.

If she could get to the cave—one she prayed was unoccupied by anything nocturnal or potentially dangerous—she might have a chance.

"Women have been giving birth by themselves for centuries," she reasoned aloud, needing to convince herself. "If they can do it, so can I."

Any other outcome was unthinkable.

A slither of pebbles was all the warning Richard got before a string of bullets erupted over his head. He dove for cover behind a cluster of thornbush, wincing when a few of the prickles scratched his face.

"I gotta say, Blackwood," Shaw hollered, "never reckoned you'd find this place."

Richard drew both Colts and cocked the hammers. "Where's my wife, Shaw?"

His hate-filled voice taunted, "Dead by now. Probably buzzard food. Her and the brat both." Laughter punctuated the cruel words.

Richard wouldn't believe that.

"Where's Evelyn?" he demanded, thinking of his sweet wife out there alone, fighting for her life and that of their child.

"You killed my brother," Shaw shouted back.

More bullets flew.

Richard ducked just in time as one pinged about a foot from his ear. Counting on the shadows to shield him, he rolled to his feet and fired several rounds through the thornbush, both Colts at once.

Richard smiled grimly at the sound of Shaw's hoarse oath.

Gotcha, you sonofabitch.

"I didn't kill your brother, the fall off the roof did." Richard reloaded and re-cocked. "Do the right thing for once in your life, Grover. Tell me where my wife is."

"Don't think I will. Think I'll just shoot you and watch you bleed. Like your woman did when I left her for dead."

Richard ground his back teeth together, fighting the intense rage Shaw's words induced. *He's lying.*

Evelyn wasn't dead. He'd somehow know if she was. *He's just trying to rattle me.*

Sucking in a deep breath, he calmed himself. This was a fight he couldn't lose. If he had any chance of rescuing his wife and child, he needed to remain levelheaded.

Grover fired off two more shots, both going wild. The man must be tiring, which made him unstable— and crafty too.

Shaw would bank on Richard's mounting worry over Evelyn to draw him out and force him to do something stupid, risky.

Not gonna happen.

Instead, he used his fear to keep his focus sharp. Crouching low, Richard eased up the trail in the encroaching darkness, battling back the urgency. If he acted impulsively now, he'd forfeit all.

One step at a time, quietly, he advanced, straining to hear any small noise that'd reveal Shaw's hiding place.

There. The sound of expelled spit, ahead and to the left.

Sure enough, Shaw stood—the outline of a single gun barely visible—smack in the middle of the trail, giving Richard the element of surprise.

With one chance and so much to lose, he sprang up and brought both barrels level, firing.

An agonized scream rent the air as Grover went down.

Holstering his weapons, Richard reached for the handcuffs clipped to his belt. Without an ounce of sympathy for the sobbing, writhing man on the ground, he strode over to his quarry and crouched next to him. Eying him dispassionately, Richard noted one shot had missed, but the other had hit right above the knee, which bled sluggishly.

Flipping Shaw onto his stomach, Richard twisted the man's hands behind his back and none-too-gently handcuffed him.

"You're done for, Shaw. You're under arrest for the murder of Judge Ezra Toomey, the suspected murder of Henry Tipple, attempted murder of Winnifred Calhoun, kidnapping, arson, and theft. I could go on, I'm sure."

Richard rose to his feet. "You might bleed out and die here. Or you might live to rot in Territorial until they plant you in the ground." He shrugged. "Hard to say."

"You can't leave me here like this!" Grover blubbered, struggling to free himself.

Richard rubbed his chin. "You're right." Spying the man's horse several yards away, he approached easily and quieted the fractious beast, finding a length of rope tied to the saddle.

He returned to Shaw with the rope and efficiently looped one end through the handcuffs, then knotted the other to his good leg, effectively hogtying him.

Shaw let out another screech.

"Shut up. I'm letting you live, you worthless pile of dung. There's a posse out searching for my wife. I'll send them over for you once she's safe." Richard pushed his face close to Shaw's. "So you'd better hope I find her. Unharmed. Because if I don't, I'll make what's left of your life hell on earth."

As he turned away, Grover shouted, "I'll take you to her, right now! Help me and I'll help you."

Richard's upper lip curled into a sneer. "I can find her myself, asshole. I don't need you anymore."

He rode away while Shaw lay in the dirt, cursing foully.

At the repugnant thought of giving birth on the bare cave floor, Evelyn had removed her dress and used it as a cushion of sorts, grateful to be out of the storm which had strengthened as night fell. Leaving her single petticoat and chemise on, she'd pulled up the yards of linen, exposing her lower half to the air.

Not wanting to attract hungry wildlife, she locked her jaw tight to hold in her screams as another pain wracked her body. Instinctively, she widened her legs as the urge to bear down became overwhelming.

What little her mother had shared regarding childbirth could probably be written on the head of a penny nail with room to spare. All the books Evelyn had read over the years while at the academy, the Latin and Greek tomes, journals in French, none of it was worth anything when compared to the knowledge she needed this very minute.

"Mama, I wish you were here," she cried out, her voice echoing weakly in the cave. *Is she even still alive?* Grief pummeled Evelyn at the thought of her mother being gone.

As perspiration drenched her body, she allowed herself to cry for a few minutes before finally drying her eyes and girding her loins.

I can do this.

She had to. She'd never let her child die. The next contraction hit with such force it was impossible to remain quiet. She screamed long and loud, discovering it helped to relieve some of the pain as she rode it out.

When the spasm finally eased, she fell back onto the damp fabric, panting. Lowering one hand to the juncture of her thighs, her fingers encountered the barest wisp of silky hair across the babe's head. "Oh, Lord, what am I supposed to do?"

"Evie! Where are you?" Richard's hoarse shout was the sweetest sound she'd ever heard.

"Here! Richard, in the cave." Evelyn struggled to one elbow, dizzy with relief. "Hurry, the babe is coming. *Now*!"

Chapter 23

When Richard found the cave entrance, the sight that met him was one he'd never forget. Moonlight shone into the shallow space, illuminating Evelyn, slumped on the rough cave floor with her petticoats bunched above her heaving belly.

Self-reproach rode him hard for allowing her to so easily be taken by Shaw. Faced with the evidence of her suffering, he had to bite down on his lip to keep his self-recriminations to himself as he closed the short distance between them. The only thing that mattered now was the safety of his wife and child.

Dropping to his knees, he gripped her hands, noting her swollen eyes, red-rimmed from crying, her face white with pain. A contraction swept over her that couldn't have been her first. As the babe undulated under her skin in its quest to be born, an agonized moan fell from her lips.

"It's too soon," she panted. "I can't stop it." Her nails dug into his palms. "Richard, I'm frightened."

"Everything will be fine." Richard leaned in and pressed his lips to her damp forehead as his concern ratcheted up. "I'm not letting anything happen to you or our babe."

Fresh tears shimmered in her eyes. "Mother. He shot my mother."

"Shh. Your mother's recovering and waiting anxiously for your return." Freeing one hand, he drew back to fumble in his trouser pocket for a matchstick. "We need more light. And some cloths. I'll have to use your petticoat. A chunk of it'll make a torch if I can find a stick."

He let go of her other hand. "I'll be right back." At her soft protest, he urged, "I promise, only long enough to find what I need."

Yet he hesitated. She looked so fragile he hated to leave her even for a moment.

"Go, but please hurry."

With a grim nod, he exited the cave. A few feet from the entrance, he spotted a patch of tall maiden grass.

It'll have to do.

Ripping up as much as he could, he bound it into three makeshift torches, using some of the twine Doc Sheaton had given him.

Hurrying to where he'd hitched Buster, he rummaged in one of the saddlebags until he found his tinderbox, grabbing both canteens as well.

Carrying it all back to the cave, he knelt next to Evelyn, who seemed to have calmed despite the circumstances. He lit the first stalk. "This might not burn long."

Hoping to hell she was well past modesty by now, he took a moment to cup her face. "We'll get through this together, Evie."

Pride filled him as her stubborn chin lifted with resolve. She nodded silently, pain and tears shimmering in her eyes.

"That's my girl," he murmured. He unscrewed the canteen and raised it to her lips. "Here, drink."

After she'd taken a few sips, he set the canteen aside, settling himself between her legs. To his amazement, he could see a delicate crown of wispy dark hair as their babe struggled to be born.

Praying that the process of birthing a child might be similar to calving, he anchored the burning stalk between a rock and the cave wall. "You'll need to push hard."

"Are you sure?" she asked faintly, weariness evident on her beautiful face.

Lord, please guide me. "I'm sure. When the next pain comes you *push.*"

Rending the petticoat in two, he soaked the fabric in water and laid it between her legs. He'd no sooner gotten it in place when she let out an ear-shattering scream, her body spasming.

"Push, Evie! Push hard," he shouted, his hands guiding first that tiny head, then the birdlike shoulders. "One more and we're there."

"I-I can't," she sobbed, trembling.

"Yes, you can. Push. Do it now!"

"Oh, God." With one final, mighty effort, she bore down, and the rest of those dainty limbs slid free.

Richard sat back on his heels, staring disbelievingly at the slippery newborn in his hands. "A girl," he marveled.

As if by instinct he held his brand-new daughter by her heels and slapped her minuscule bottom, eliciting a sudden, indignant cry. "Oh, love, you did it. We have a girl!"

Using the damp cloth as protection from the cave floor, he laid the babe down and cleaned out her nose and mouth, then wiped her off. Remembering Doc's instructions, he fumbled for the twine and knife in his pocket, tying off the cord connecting their babe to her mother in two places and slicing between. The last dry piece of petticoat was enough to swaddle her.

"Evie, she's perfect."

She didn't answer.

"Evie?" When he looked up and saw how she slumped on the ground, a growing stain of red under her hips, fear choked his breath. "Evelyn!"

Her eyes fluttered open. "I don't feel good, Mama."

Then she fainted.

Evelyn came to gradually, cradled in strong arms.

Every bone in her body ached, the pain echoing in her muscles. Inside she felt strangely empty. She raised a hand to push her matted hair aside, and encountered a warmth snuggled against her chest.

Hesitantly, she touched the satin skin, the soft-as-gossamer head. Shifting to get her first look at the infant suckling at her breast, she cried out as her body trembled with residual pain from the hard labor.

"Shh, don't move, love. I've got you both," Richard murmured.

The endearment stole her heart.

"You slept for a while right after her birth." He trailed a finger over their daughter's cheek. "You scared me to death."

"I'm so weak," she whispered. Feeling a soggy lump between her legs, she stared blearily at the stained cloth. "That's blood."

"I know. The bleeding stopped a little while ago, after you expelled what kept our child safe in your womb. In calving we call it afterbirth. Don't rightly know what it's called for a woman."

She wrinkled her nose but managed a smile. "I don't rightly know, either." Relaxing, she cupped their daughter's head. "Is she healthy?"

"Yep. I counted her fingers and toes. I got her to latch on too. Tiny, but she's a scrapper." He kissed her hair. "Nice work, Mama."

Weary but insanely happy, Evelyn yawned and closed her eyes. "You too, Papa."

Richard dozed in fits and starts, waking each time Evelyn did or whenever their daughter emitted any noise at all. As the night wore on, the storm lessened until stopping completely, shortly before sunrise. Although the air remained uncomfortably muggy, a morning chill settled inside the damp cave.

Ensuring the safety of his family became a breathing, living thing inside him. Even knowing Evelyn needed to rest from her ordeal, he had no choice but to set out today for Little Creede to get them both the medical attention they needed.

Thankfully, he'd been able to coax a few swallows of water down her throat each time she woke, and he prayed it would help her regain some strength for the arduous journey.

Staring out from the cave entrance, he also prayed when the time came to move her, she wouldn't start bleeding again. That was more worrisome than anything else. With no knowledge of what was normal for birthing mothers, his growing concern had no outlet.

Evelyn's hoarse whisper broke the silence. "Richard?"

He brushed a kiss on her bare shoulder. "I'm here."

"The babe. She needs a name. In case I don't—"

"Hush, now." He couldn't bear to hear the rest. "We're going to leave here together."

"I'm still bleeding. That's not normal."

"Sweetheart, neither of us knows what is normal and what isn't. All we know is our child came early, she's able to nurse, and you need more sleep."

He cradled her, refusing to think of any consequence other than—God willing—years of happiness with her and the children they'd be blessed with.

Desperate to distract her from such dismal thoughts, he asked, "What names do you like?"

Silence.

"Evie? Love?"

She'd fallen asleep again, limp and breathing deeply. Closing his eyes against their stinging burn, he buried his face in her tangled hair. "Rest, Evie."

Richard bit his lip until he tasted blood. At the thought of losing his precious wife, anguish tightened his chest. "I love you so much," he declared aloud, knowing it to be true.

A murmur was his only answer.

Their daughter chose that moment to waken and emit a thin wail, her rosebud mouth losing the nipple. Cupping her fragile head, he guided the infant back to her mother's breast, waiting as she rooted fretfully before finding nourishment with a grunt.

"There, little one. Eat your dinner." Holding his family close, he sent a few more prayers heavenward. "I'm going to take such good care of you and your mama." Wide-awake, he watched the sunrise filter over the land.

Somewhere below Bear Rock, the posse Ben had promised to organize must be searching for them. With some of the ground softened from rain, Richard could only hope enough of Buster's tracks would be left behind.

If not, he'd have to find a way to get them home himself.

Evelyn stirred in his arms. "Shh," he murmured. "Go back to sleep."

"Where are we?" She raised her face to his. He winced at her sunken cheeks, visible in the growing light.

"Still in the cave," he replied. "How do you feel?"

"Better, I think. Though I do ache all over." She peered down at their slumbering child. "Has she woken at all? Is she well?" She rubbed carefully over the minute shoulders. "So soft."

Her eyes filled with tears as she met Richard's tender regard. "Can we keep her safe? A helpless little mite in a rough mining town. I've t-tried hard to adapt and be courageous. But what if that awful man comes looking for us?"

At least he could allay those fears. "Floyd Shaw is dead, and Grover can't bother us anymore. I left him wounded and hogtied. The town law will come for him. He'll stand trial in either Silver Cache or

Georgetown, then he'll be incarcerated at Territorial Prison for the rest of his miserable life."

Contempt roughened his tone. "If he isn't hanged first for murder."

"Good riddance."

In those two words Richard heard new-mama ferociousness. "I fully agree."

She chewed on her bottom lip as she stared at him.

He arched one brow. "What is it?"

"Um." Evelyn blushed, looking shy. "I don't know if I was dreaming." She emitted a short laugh. "But I thought I heard you say . . ."

Richard lowered his lips to hers for a soft, tender kiss. Finally, he pulled back to stare into her pretty blue eyes. "You heard me say that I love you, Missus Blackwood."

Happiness seemed to set her aglow. "Do you, Richard? Do you love me?"

"I do, Evie. I think I fell in love with you back in Baltimore. Unfortunately, I can be thickheaded at times and didn't recognize the emotion." He swept a lock of hair off her cheek. "Now I do. You and our beautiful daughter mean everything to me."

"I love you too, Richard. Though I was too much of a coward to admit it back then, even to myself."

Her brows furrowed. "I didn't want to lose my father's affection." A fierce expression flashed across her face, then fell away. "I didn't understand I never had it to start."

"I'm sorry."

She laid a finger over his mouth. "No." She beamed up at him. "What I didn't realize then is that I don't need his approval. All I need is you. My kind, caring, brave husband."

Her loving gaze fell to the miracle they'd created. "And our daughter. Isn't she adorable?"

It wasn't really a question.

Richard raised Evelyn's chin, tilting her face back to him. "She is, just like her mother." Unable to resist, he leaned in to taste her lips again.

When their babe started to fuss, Evelyn broke away. "She's wet, Richard."

"Doubtful she minds."

"We can't keep calling her *she*. We need a proper name for our little angel." She rocked their daughter carefully, cradling her soggy little bottom. "We could name her Angela. After Saint Angela de Merici."

The name was familiar. "If I recall my catechism, she was a patron of determination and strength." A grin spread over his face. "I think Angela Blackwood is perfect."

"Blackwood!" The shout echoed in the early-morning stillness.

Evelyn gasped, clutching Angela so tightly, she woke and let out an indignant wail. "Richard, who—"

"Easy, love." He rose and peered out the mouth of the cave, relieved beyond measure to see the approaching riders. "We're safe now."

EPILOGUE

Evelyn brought her daughter to her shoulder and rubbed her back, coaxing a burp that vibrated through the babe, accompanied by a definite milk-toot.

"What a good girl you are," she crooned, then waved her hand in front of her nose. "Smelly too." She nuzzled Angela's downy head. "I don't mind," she whispered in mother love, rocking gently.

Richard sank down onto the sofa next to her, hugging her close. "All finished?"

"Your daughter is a little piggy." At his chuckle, Evelyn sighed in bliss. "She's gained some much-needed weight."

He stroked his thumb over Angela's satiny cheek. "She'll look like her mama."

"Not with such dark hair." Evelyn lifted her face for his kiss. "Spitting image of her papa," she murmured against his lips.

He rubbed noses with her teasingly. "Half you and half me."

In the shadowy, early-morning room they sat quietly, watching their child slumbering.

Evelyn stifled a yawn. "I don't know why I'm still this tired."

"You could ask your mother how she felt after giving birth." He leaned his head back against the sofa cushion. "I imagine she experienced the same with you."

"Actually, when I was newly-born, I had a wet nurse," Evelyn mused. "It was the thing to do among the high society set. And a nanny. Mother seemed a trifle guilty when she admitted she'd never changed a single diaper. I've been almost afraid to ask her to change Angela's."

"You need to involve her as much as you can. It'll be good for her to learn, seeing as we plan to provide her with several more grandchildren." He sent her a lusty wink. "I have a fierce need of you."

Remembering the fortune teller's reading, a smile broke across her face. "Seven."

Confusion furrowed his brow. "What?"

"Madame Zoee told me we'd have a house full of children someday. Seven to be exact."

He grunted. "I'm not normally one to believe such things, but without her help I might've never found you. So it looks like I'll need to add more rooms onto the ranch."

Fingering the button on his shirt, she cast him a flirtatious look. "When can we start?"

His gaze darkened. "As soon as you feel well enough, love." He tenderly traced her throat.

Angela chose that moment to awaken and whimper, tiny fists flailing. "Somebody's hungry again," Evelyn declared, resigned at the interruption yet thrilled at their daughter's healthy appetite.

She loosened the front of her nightshift and guided the ravenous infant to her breast. "Talk to me while she nurses. What's the latest town gossip?"

Richard toyed with a lock of her hair. "With how busy our little girl kept us last night, it completely slipped my mind. A telegram came in before I left for home. One of the guards over at the Georgetown jail reported Grover Shaw had been killed."

She gasped. "How?"

"Apparently someone entered his cell in the middle of the night and stabbed him to death."

"Good Lord." She crossed herself out of habit. "Any clue as to why?"

"They owed a crime family in Chicago a considerable amount of money. We figure the organization was behind it."

"But in Georgetown? How would they know either brother would be there and not somewhere else?"

"Rail reservations can be accessed if you know who to ask and how much of a bribe to offer. The stage from Denver keeps a record of passengers."

Richard reached for Angela, drowsy again. He propped her on his shoulder and gently worked out a few burps. "I'm going to tuck our little princess into her cradle. If she's wet, I'll change her."

Yawning, Evelyn relaxed against the sofa cushions. Doc Sheaton had made her promise to rest when she could.

Her eyes fluttered closed for a few moments of blessed rest before she sat up abruptly. "How could I forget Granny Nia's birthday?"

The celebration was taking place this afternoon at the Galleria, with family on both sides invited, including Robert and his wife and son, currently visiting from Silver Cache.

"So much for napping." Sighing, Evelyn struggled to her feet.

Later that afternoon, buggies and buckboards lined both sides of the widened road near the Galleria.

Clutching her husband's coat sleeve, Evelyn paused on the expansive front porch, breathing in the early-autumn air. Over her arm she held a basket containing Angela's extra diapers and a change of clothing, plus a small, stitched sampler she had made for Granny Nia as a birthday gift. Against Richard's shoulder, Angela dozed fitfully.

The noise level beyond the double doors attested to the size of the crowd inside, children shrieking amidst the adult chatter.

Couples gathered in the casino lobby, their offspring darting about, chasing each other. A few of the younger girls fussed with dolls.

In one corner Nate patiently held a length of twine, trying to teach Retta's boys how to play cat's cradle, while Addie and her sister Jenny took turns with a bilbo ball and cup.

Evelyn stretched on her toes to peer over the melee. "I can't see the guest of honor anywhere. Ah, there she is." She pointed toward a parlor to the left of the lobby where Granny Nia happily perched on a wide settee, Retta's youngest girl, Quinn on one knee and Isiah on the other. "She's in her glory now."

Both tots seemed to be behaving themselves well enough, with the added support of Richard's aunt close by. Behind the settee, Harrison and Joshua chatted quietly.

When Lucinda turned to whisper something to her mother-by-marriage, Granny Nia leaned her silvery head on Lucinda's shoulder. The proud old woman's smile revealed such contentment.

"I don't want to disturb her when she's got a lapful of grand-babes and your aunt's excellent company." Evelyn smoothed her skirts, catching Richard's nod of agreement. "Perhaps we can wait a bit before offering our well-wishes."

Spotting her mother entering the salon, Evelyn waved her over.

"Sweetheart." Mother came to them with graceful strides, glowing in creamy lace-over-satin. "There you are." Her eyes latched on to Angela, who'd begun to stir. "How is my darling grandchild?" She held out her arms. "I would love to cuddle her."

Without hesitation Richard handed off their daughter who stared at her granny for a second or two, then released a hearty wail.

"She needs to be changed," he commented, as Mother wrinkled her nose at the odor emanating from Angela's bulging diaper.

"I'm not, I never—" She floundered. "Evelyn?"

Stifling the urge to laugh, Evelyn took pity on her. "Come on, I'll help you." She led the way to a corner of the room, blessedly quiet, where an elegant chesterfield sat. Opening her basket, she pulled out a soft piece of flannel and spread it out. "Lay her on this."

Gingerly, Mother did as she bade. "She might roll off."

"Which is why you put your palm on her chest, thusly." Evelyn demonstrated, waiting until her mother copied her before stepping back.

"You must think me a complete ninny."

"Of course I don't. I think your upbringing never afforded you much of an opportunity." Evelyn dug out a diaper and passed it over, touching her mother's fingers reassuringly. "How wonderful you'll get that chance with your first grandchild." She paused. "Maybe more."

"More?" Mother looked scandalized. "You're not already with—"

"*No.*" Still, Evelyn couldn't resist teasing, "But you know, when a man and a woman love each other very much . . ." She trailed off at the brilliant red staining her mother's cheeks. "You should see your face," she exclaimed, and burst into laughter.

For a moment Mother looked indignant, then her humor surfaced, and she joined in. Their mirth pealed from the corner of the parlor, while Angela kicked her legs and gurgled.

Richard nudged his brother in the ribs as their granny crooned to Angela who rested in her embrace, staring up as if fascinated.

"She's in grandchild heaven," he commented.

"Yep." Robert raised his tumbler of lemonade in a toast. "And many more, I say."

Over the low chatter of dinner conversation, Granny hummed, a gnarled finger clasped in Angela's chubby fist. "You'll be a feisty one, for certain," she rasped softly. "Got a grip like I once had." She leaned in and kissed the babe's dark tuft.

In answer, Angela blew a noisy milk bubble, causing Granny to cackle in delight. "You tell 'em, sweet child." She looked up at first Richard, then Robert, a sly expression on her wrinkled face. "Going to give me more of these rascals, ain't you?"

"Yes, ma'am," they responded in unison.

"Don't think I won't hold you to it. And be quick about it, I won't live forever." She returned her attention to the bundle on her lap, rearing aside when Angela swung a fist, narrowly missing an eye. "She's a Blackwood, all right."

Richard cast his attention over the rest of the table's occupants, his gaze settling on Evelyn's mama, who was proving to be a revelation.

Thanks to her daughter's endless patience, Winnifred had managed a creditable diaper change. After learning of her privileged life in East Coast society, he better understood how the lack of simple life lessons had robbed the woman of so many joys.

At her side, Ike Barnes alternated between conversing genially with Frank Carter, seated nearby, and gazing fondly at Winnifred, causing her to blush.

Richard glanced at his wife to see if she'd noticed and caught her curious regard. For weeks now, he'd had a suspicion Evelyn's mother and Ike might have developed some tender feelings toward each other and thought it grand how two lonely people might find happiness together.

He filled his plate with a second serving of dessert. "This cobbler is superb. Dolores outdid herself."

Winnifred cleared her throat delicately. "I brought it."

"Mother, you made this?" Evelyn laid her fork on her empty plate. "When did you learn how to bake?"

"Well. . ." Mother glanced sideways at Ike. "Mister Barnes assisted, um, taught me."

"Did he, now?" Richard murmured, biting back a grin.

"How exactly did you assist my mother?"

A faint smile accompanied Ike's smooth response. "I'm happy to teach the lovely Winnie anytime."

Evelyn's brows crawled up to her hairline. "*Winnie?*"

Catherine chose that moment to interrupt. "Time for gifts."

Without another word, Ike rose to help Winnifred to her feet.

Richard also stood to assist Evelyn, whose sharp gaze bounced between her mother and Ike before meeting his. "What do you think?"

"I think Ike is smitten, and your mother will eventually catch up."

As Evelyn watched the two walk away together, her eyes sparkled that deep, deep blue he loved so much.

She squeezed his arm. "Oh, this is going to be so much fun."

Thank You from CiCi Cordelia

Dear Reader,

Thank you for joining us on this thrilling journey through the silver-rich hills of Colorado. Your support and enthusiasm for the BRIDES OF LITTLE CREEDE series mean the world to us. We hope these stories of love, courage, and new beginnings have touched your heart and transported you to a time of adventure and romance.

We invite you to continue the adventure with the complete BRIDES OF LITTLE CREEDE series. Each book offers a unique tale of love and perseverance in the Old West, but together they weave a rich tapestry of interconnected lives and shared dreams.

You can find the complete Brides of Little Creede series

on Amazon. Just search for CiCi Cordelia!

Discover More:

We'd love for you to explore more of our work and stay connected.

Here's how you can do that:

🌐 Visit our website: **CiCiWriter.com** – Where we are _Writing from the Heart_

▨ Find us on Facebook:

📷 Connect with us on Instagram: https://www.instagram.com/cicicordduet/

Thank you again for being a part of our Little Creede family. We hope you'll continue to join us for more thrilling tales of love and adventure in the Old West!

With gratitude,

Char & Cheryl, writing as CiCi Cordelia